LIMEHOUSE

ALSO BY THOMAS BURKE

LIMEHOUSE NIGHTS

THOMAS BURKE

WILDSIDE PRESS

To Caradoc Evans

LIMEHOUSE NIGHTS

Published by
Wildside Press
P.O. Box 301
Holicong, PA 18928-0301 USA
www.wildsidepress.com

CONTENTS

THE CHINK AND THE CHILD

IT is a tale of love and lovers that they tell in the low-lit Causeway that slinks from West India Dock Road to the dark waste of waters beyond. In Pennyfields, too, you may hear it; and I do not doubt that it is told in far-away Tai-Ping, in Singapore, in Tokyo, in Shanghai, and those other gay-lamped haunts of wonder whither the wandering people of Limehouse go and whence they return so casually. It is a tale for tears, and should you hear it in the lilied tongue of the yellow men, it would awaken in you all your pity. In our bald speech it must, unhappily, lose its essential fragrance, that quality that will lift an affair of squalor into the loftier spheres of passion and imagination, beauty and sorrow. It will sound unconvincing, a little . . . you know . . . the kind of thing that is best forgotten. Perhaps . . .

But listen.

It is Battling Burrows, the lightning welterweight of Shadwell, the box o' tricks, the Tetrarch of the ring, who enters first. Battling Burrows, the pride of Ratcliff, Poplar and Limehouse, and the despair of his manager and backers. For he loved wine, woman and song; and the boxing world held that he couldn't last long on that. There was any amount of money in him for his parasites if only the damned women could be cut out; but again and again would he disappear from his training quarters on the eve of a big fight, to consort with Molly and Dolly, and to drink other things than barley-water and lemon-juice. Wherefore Chuck Lightfoot, his manager, forced him to fight on any and every occasion while he was good and a money-maker; for at any moment the collapse might come, and Chuck would be called upon by his creditors to strip off that "shirt" which at every contest he laid upon his man.

Battling was of a type that is too common in the eastern districts of London; a type that upsets all accepted classifications. He wouldn't be classed. He was a curious mixture of athleticism and degeneracy. He could run like a deer, leap like a greyhound, fight like a machine, and drink like a suction-hose. He was a bully; he had the courage of the high hero. He was an open-air sport; he had the vices of a French decadent.

It was one of his love adventures that properly begins this tale; for the girl had come to Battling one night with a recital of terrible happenings, of an angered parent, of a slammed door. . . . In her arms was a bundle of white rags. Now Battling, like so many sensualists, was also a sentimen-

7

talist. He took that bundle of white rags; he paid the girl money to get into the country; and the bundle of white rags had existed in and about his domicile in Pekin Street, Limehouse, for some eleven years. Her position was nondescript; to the casual observer it would seem that she was Battling's relief punch-ball—an unpleasant post for any human creature to occupy, especially if you are a little girl of twelve, and the place be the one-room household of the lightning welter-weight. When Battling was cross with his manager . . . well, it is indefensible to strike your manager or to throw chairs at him, if he is a good manager; but to use a dog-whip on a small child is permissible and quite as satisfying; at least, he found it so. On these occasions, then, when very cross with his sparring partners, or over-flushed with victory and juice of the grape, he would flog Lucy. But he was reputed by the boys to be a good fellow. He only whipped the child when he was drunk; and he was only drunk for eight months of the year.

For just over twelve years this bruised little body had crept about Poplar and Limehouse. Always the white face was scarred with red, or black-furrowed with tears; always in her steps and in her look was expectation of dread things. Night after night her sleep was broken by the cheerful Battling's brute voice and violent hands; and terrible were the lessons which life taught her in those few years. Yet, for all the starved face and the transfixed air, there was a lurking beauty about her, a something that called you in the soft curve of her cheek that cried for kisses and was fed with blows, and in the splendid mournfulness that grew in eyes and lips. The brown hair chimed against the pale face, like the rounding of a verse. The blue cotton frock and the broken shoes could not break the loveliness of her slender figure or the shy grace of her movements as she flitted about the squalid alleys of the docks; though in all that region of wasted life and toil and decay, there was not one that noticed her, until . . .

Now there lived in Chinatown, in one lousy room over Mr. Tai Fu's store in Pennyfields, a wandering yellow man named Cheng Huan. Cheng Huan was a poet. He did not realise it. He had never been able to understand why he was unpopular; and he died without knowing. But a poet he was, tinged with the materialism of his race, and in his poor listening heart strange echoes would awake of which he himself was barely conscious. He regarded things differently from other sailors; he felt things more passionately, and things which they felt not at all; so he lived alone instead of at one of the lodging-houses. Every evening he would sit at his window and watch the street. Then, a little later, he would take a jolt of opium at the place at the corner of Formosa Street.

He had come to London by devious ways. He had loafed on the Bund at Shanghai. The fateful intervention of a crimp had landed him on a boat. He got to Cardiff, and sojourned in its Chinatown; thence to Liverpool, to Glasgow; thence, by a ticket from the Asiatics' Aid Society, to Limehouse, where he remained for two reasons—because it cost him nothing to live there, and because he was too lazy to find a boat to take him back to Shanghai.

So he would lounge and smoke cheap cigarettes, and sit at his window, from which point he had many times observed the lyrical Lucy. He noticed her casually. Another day, he observed her, not casually. Later, he looked long at her; later still, he began to watch for her and for that strangely provocative something about the toss of the head and the hang of the little blue skirt as it coyly kissed her knee.

Then that beauty which all Limehouse had missed smote Cheng. Straight to his heart it went, and cried itself into his very blood. Thereafter the spirit of poetry broke her blossoms all about his odorous chamber. Nothing was the same. Pennyfields became a happy-lanterned street, and the monotonous fiddle in the house opposite was the music of his fathers. Bits of old song floated through his mind: little sweet verses of Le Tai-pih, murmuring of plum blossom, ricefield and stream. Day by day he would moon at his window, or shuffle about the streets, lighting to a flame when Lucy would pass and gravely return his quiet regard; and night after night, too, he would dream of a pale, lily-lovely child.

And now the Fates moved swiftly various pieces on their sinister board, and all that followed happened with a speed and precision that showed direction from higher ways.

It was Wednesday night in Limehouse, and for once clear of mist. Out of the coloured darkness of the Causeway stole the muffled wail of reed instruments, and, though every window was closely shuttered, between the joints shot jets of light and stealthy voices, and you could hear the whisper of slippered feet, and the stuttering steps of the satyr and the sadist. It was to the café in the middle of the Causeway, lit by the pallid blue light that is the symbol of China throughout the world, that Cheng Huan came, to take a dish of noodle and some tea. Thence he moved to another house whose stairs ran straight to the street, and above whose doorway a lamp glowed like an evil eye. At this establishment he mostly took his pipe of "chandu" and a brief chat with the keeper of the house, for, although not popular, and very silent, he liked sometimes to be in the presence of his compatriots. Like a figure of a shadowgraph he slid through the door and up the stairs.

The chamber he entered was a bit of the Orient squatting at the portals of the West. It was a well-kept place where one might play a game of fan-tan, or take a shot or so of *li-un*, or purchase other varieties of Oriental delight. It was sunk in a purple dusk, though here and there a lantern stung the glooms. Low couches lay around the walls, and strange men decorated them: Chinese, Japs, Malays, Lascars, with one or two white girls; and sleek, noiseless attendants swam from couch to couch. Away in the far corner sprawled a lank figure in brown shirting, its nerveless fingers curled about the stem of a spent pipe. On one of the lounges a scorbutic negro sat with a Jewess from Shadwell. Squatting on a table in the centre, beneath one of the lanterns, was a musician with a reed, blinking upon the company like a sly cat and making his melody of six repeated notes.

The atmosphere churned. The dirt of years, tobacco of many growings, opium, betel nut, and moist flesh allied themselves in one grand assault against the nostrils.

As Cheng brooded on his insect-ridden cushion, of a sudden the lantern above the musician was caught by the ribbon of his reed. It danced and flung a hazy radiance on a divan in the shadow. He saw—started—half rose. His heart galloped, and the blood pounded in his quiet veins. Then he dropped again, crouched, and stared.

O lily-flowers and plum blossoms! O silver streams and dim-starred skies! O wine and roses, song and laughter! For there, kneeling on a mass of rugs, mazed and big-eyed, but understanding, was Lucy . . . his Lucy . . . his little maid. Through the dusk she must have felt his intent gaze upon her; for he crouched there, fascinated, staring into the now obscured corner where she knelt.

But the sickness which momentarily gripped him on finding in this place his snowy-breasted pearl passed and gave place to great joy. She was here; he would talk with her. Little English he had, but simple words, those with few gutturals, he had managed to pick up; so he rose, the masterful lover, and, with feline movements, crossed the nightmare chamber to claim his own.

If you wonder how Lucy came to be in this bagnio, the explanation is simple. Battling was in training. He had flogged her that day before starting work; he had then had a few brandies—not many; some eighteen or nineteen—and had locked the door of his room and taken the key. Lucy was, therefore, homeless, and a girl somewhat older than Lucy, so old and so wise, as girls are in that region, saw in her a possible source of revenue.

So there they were, and to them appeared Cheng.

From what horrors he saved her that night cannot be told, for her ways were too audaciously childish to hold her long from harm in such a place. What he brought to her was love and death.

For he sat by her. He looked at her—reverently yet passionately. He touched her—wistfully yet eagerly. He locked a finger in her wondrous hair. She did not start away; she did not tremble. She knew well what she had to be afraid of in that place; but she was not afraid of Cheng. She pierced the mephitic gloom and scanned his face. No, she was not afraid. His yellow hands, his yellow face, his smooth black hair . . . well, he was the first thing that had ever spoken soft words to her; the first thing that had ever laid a hand upon her that was not brutal; the first thing that had deferred in manner towards her as though she, too, had a right to live. She knew his words were sweet, though she did not understand them. Nor can they be set down. Half that he spoke was in village Chinese; the rest in a mangling of English which no distorted spelling could possibly reproduce.

But he drew her back against the cushions and asked her name, and she told him; and he inquired her age, and she told him; and he had then two beautiful words which came easily to his tongue. He repeated them again and again:

"Lucia . . . li'l Lucia. . . . Twelve. . . . Twelve." Musical phrases they were, dropping from his lips, and to the child who heard her name pronounced so lovingly, they were the lost heights of melody. She clung to him, and he to her. She held his strong arm in both of hers as they crouched on the divan, and nestled her cheek against his coat.

Well . . . he took her home to his wretched room.

"Li'l Lucia, come-a-home . . . Lucia."

His heart was on fire. As they slipped out of the noisomeness into the night air and crossed the West India Dock Road into Pennyfields, they passed unnoticed. It was late, for one thing, and for another . . . well, nobody cared particularly. His blood rang with soft music and the solemnity of drums, for surely he had found now what for many years he had sought—his world's one flower. Wanderer he was, from Tuan-tsen to Shanghai, Shanghai to Glasgow . . . Cardiff . . . Liverpool . . . London. He had dreamed often of the women of his native land; perchance one of them should be his flower. Women, indeed, there had been. Swatow . . . he had recollections of certain rose-winged hours in coast cities. At many places to which chance had led him a little bird had perched itself upon his heart, but so lightly and for so brief a while as hardly to be felt. But now—now he had found her in this alabaster Cockney child. So that he was glad and had great joy of himself and the blue and silver night, and the harsh flares of the Poplar Hippodrome.

You will observe that he had claimed her, but had not asked himself whether she were of an age for love. The white perfection of the child had captivated every sense. It may be that he forgot that he was in London and not in Tuan-tsen. It may be that he did not care. Of that nothing can be told. All that is known is that his love was a pure and holy thing. Of that we may be sure, for his worst enemies have said it.

Slowly, softly they mounted the stairs to his room, and with almost an obeisance he entered and drew her in. A bank of cloud raced to the east and a full moon thrust a sharp sword of light upon them. Silence lay over all Pennyfields. With a birdlike movement, she looked up at him—her face alight, her tiny hands upon his coat—clinging, wondering, trusting. He took her hand and kissed it; repeated the kiss upon her cheek and lip and little bosom, twining his fingers in her hair. Docilely, and echoing the smile of his lemon lips in a way that thrilled him almost to laughter, she returned his kisses impetuously, gladly.

He clasped the nestling to him. Bruised, tearful, with the love of life almost thrashed out of her, she had fluttered to him out of the evil night.

"O li'l Lucia!" And he put soft hands upon her, and smoothed her and crooned over her many gracious things in his flowered speech. So they stood in the moonlight, while she told him the story of her father, of her beatings, and starvings, and unhappiness.

"O li'l Lucia. . . . White Blossom. . . . Twelve. . . . Twelve years old!"

As he spoke, the clock above the Milwall Docks shot twelve crashing notes across the night. When the last echo died, he moved to a cupboard, and from it he drew strange things . . . formless masses of blue and gold, magical things of silk, and a vessel that was surely Aladdin's lamp, and a box of spices. He took these robes, and, with tender, reverent fingers, removed from his White Blossom the besmirched rags that covered her, and robed her again, and led her then to the heap of stuff that was his bed, and bestowed her safely.

For himself, he squatted on the floor before her, holding one grubby little hand. There he crouched all night, under the lyric moon, sleepless, watchful; and sweet content was his. He had fallen into an uncomfortable posture, and his muscles ached intolerably. But she slept, and he dared not move nor release her hand lest he should awaken her. Weary and trustful, she slept, knowing that the yellow man was kind and that she might sleep with no fear of a steel hand smashing the delicate structure of her dreams.

In the morning, when she awoke, still wearing her blue and yellow silk, she gave a cry of amazement. Cheng had been about. Many times had he glided up and down the two flights of stairs, and now at last his room was prepared for his princess. It was swept and garnished, and was an apartment worthy a maid who is loved by a poet-prince. There was a bead curtain. There were muslins of pink and white. There were four bowls of flowers, clean, clear flowers to gladden the White Blossom and set off her sharp beauty. And there was a bowl of water, and a sweet lotion for the bruise on her cheek.

When she had risen, her prince ministered to her with rice and egg and tea. Cleansed and robed and calm, she sat before him, perched on the edge of many cushions as on a throne, with all the grace of the child princess in the story. She was a poem. The beauty hidden by neglect and fatigue shone out now more clearly and vividly, and from the head sunning over with curls to the small white feet, now bathed and sandalled, she seemed the living interpretation of a Chinese lyric. And she was his; her sweet self and her prattle, and her birdlike ways were all his own.

Oh, beautifully they loved. For two days he held her. Soft caresses from his yellow hands and long, devout kisses were all their demonstration. Each night he would tend her, as might mother to child; and each night he watched and sometimes slumbered at the foot of her couch.

But now there were those that ran to Battling at his training quarters across the river, with the news that his child had gone with a Chink—a yellow man. And Battling was angry. He discovered parental rights. He discovered indignation. A yellow man after his kid! He'd learn him. Battling did not like men who were not born in the same great country as himself. Particularly he disliked yellow men. His birth and education in Shadwell had taught him that of all creeping things that creep upon the earth the most insidious is the Oriental in the West. And a yellow man and a child. It was . . . as you might say . . . so . . . kind of . . . well, wasn't it? He bellowed that it was "unnacherel." The yeller man would go through it. Yeller! It was his supreme condemnation, his final epithet for all conduct of which he disapproved.

There was no doubt that he was extremely annoyed. He went to the Blue Lantern, in what was once Ratcliff Highway, and thumped the bar, and made all his world agree with him. And when they agreed with him he got angrier still. So that when, a few hours later, he climbed through the ropes at the Netherlands to meet Bud Tuffit for ten rounds, it was Bud's fight all the time, and to that bright boy's astonishment he was the victor on points at the end of the ten. Battling slouched out of the ring, still more determined to let the Chink have it where the chicken had the axe. He left the house with two pals and a black man, and a number of really inspired curses from his manager.

On the evening of the third day, then, Cheng slipped sleepily down the stairs to procure more flowers and more rice. The genial Ho Ling, who keeps the Canton store, held him in talk some little while, and he was gone from his room perhaps half-an-hour. Then he glided back, and climbed with happy feet the forty stairs to his temple of wonder.

With a push of a finger he opened the door, and the blood froze on his cheek, the flowers fell from him. The temple was empty and desolate; White Blossom was gone. The muslin hangings were torn down and trampled underfoot. The flowers had been flung from their bowls about the floor, and the bowls lay in fifty fragments. The joss was smashed. The cupboard had been opened. Rice was scattered here and there. The little straight bed had been jumped upon by brute feet. Everything that could be smashed or violated had been so treated, and—horror of all—the blue and yellow silk robe had been rent in pieces, tied in grotesque knots, and slung derisively about the table legs.

I pray devoutly that you may never suffer what Cheng Huan suffered in that moment. The pangs of death, with no dying; the sickness of the soul which longs to escape and cannot; the imprisoned animal within the breast which struggles madly for a voice and finds none; all the agonies of all the ages—the agonies of every abandoned lover and lost woman, past and to come—all these things were his in that moment.

Then he found voice and gave a great cry, and men from below came up to him; and they told him how the man who boxed had been there with a black man; how he had torn the robes from his child, and dragged her down the stairs by her hair; and how he had shouted aloud for Cheng and had vowed to return and deal separately with him.

Now a terrible dignity came to Cheng, and the soul of his great fathers swept over him. He closed the door against them, and fell prostrate over what had been the resting-place of White Blossom. Those without heard strange sounds as of an animal in its last pains; and it was even so. Cheng was dying. The sacrament of his high and holy passion had been profaned; the last sanctuary of the Oriental—his soul dignity—had been assaulted. The love robes had been torn to ribbons; the veil of his temple cut down. Life was no longer possible; and life without his little lady, his White Blossom, was no longer desirable.

Prostrate he lay for the space of some five minutes. Then, in his face all the pride of accepted destiny, he arose. He drew together the little bed. With reverent hands he took the pieces of blue and yellow silk, kissing them and fondling them and placing them about the pillow. Silently he gathered up the flowers, and the broken earthenware, and burnt some prayer papers and prepared himself for death.

Now it is the custom among those of the sect of Cheng that the dying shall present love-gifts to their enemies; and when he had set all in order, he gathered his brown canvas coat about him, stole from the house, and set out to find Battling Burrows, bearing under the coat his love-gift to Battling. White Blossom he had no hope of finding. He had heard of Burrows many times; and he judged that, now that she was taken from him, never again would he hold those hands or touch that laughing hair. Nor, if he did, could it change things from what they were. Nothing that was not a dog could live in the face of this sacrilege.

As he came before the house in Pekin Street, where Battling lived, he murmured gracious prayers. Fortunately, it was a night of thick river mist, and through the enveloping velvet none could observe or challenge him. The main door was open, as are all doors in this district. He writhed across the step, and through to the back room, where again the door yielded to a touch.

Darkness. Darkness and silence, and a sense of frightful things. He peered through it. Then he fumbled under his jacket—found a match—struck it. An inch of candle stood on the mantelshelf. He lit it. He looked round. No sign of Burrows, but . . . Almost before he looked he knew what awaited him. But the sense of finality had kindly stunned him; he could suffer nothing more.

On the table lay a dog-whip. In the corner a belt had been flung. Half across the greasy couch lay White Blossom. A few rags of clothing were about her pale, slim body; her hair hung limp as her limbs; her eyes were closed. As Cheng drew nearer and saw the savage red rails that ran across and across the beloved body, he could not scream—he could not think. He dropped beside the couch. He laid gentle hands upon her, and called soft names. She was warm to the touch. The pulse was still.

Softly, oh, so softly, he bent over the little frame that had enclosed his friend-spirit, and his light kisses fell all about her. Then, with the undirected movements of a sleepwalker, he bestowed the rags decently about her, clasped her in strong arms, and crept silently into the night.

From Pekin Street to Pennyfields it is but a turn or two, and again he passed unobserved as he bore his tired bird back to her nest. He laid her upon the bed, and covered the lily limbs with the blue and yellow silks and strewed upon her a few of the trampled flowers. Then, with more kisses and prayers, he crouched beside her.

So, in the ghastly Limehouse morning, they were found—the dead child, and the Chink, kneeling beside her, with a sharp knife gripped in a vicelike hand, its blade far between his ribs.

Meantime, having vented his wrath on his prodigal daughter, Battling, still cross, had returned to the Blue Lantern, and there he stayed with a brandy tumbler in his fist, forgetful of an appointment at Premierland, whereby he should have been in the ring at ten o'clock sharp. For the space of an hour Chuck Lightfoot was going blasphemously to and fro in Poplar, seeking Battling and not finding him, and murmuring, in tearful tones: "Battling—you dammanblasted Battling—where are yeh?"

His opponent was in his corner sure enough, but there was no fight. For Battling lurched from the Blue Lantern to Pekin Street. He lurched into his happy home, and he cursed Lucy, and called for her. And finding no matches, he lurched to where he knew the couch should be, and flopped heavily down.

Now it is a peculiarity of the reptile tribe that its members are impatient of being flopped on without warning. So, when Battling flopped, eighteen inches of writhing gristle upreared itself on the couch, and got home on him as Bud Tuffit had done the night before—one to the ear, one to the throat, and another to the forearm.

Battling went down and out.

And he, too, was found in the morning, with Cheng Huan's love-gift coiled about his neck.

THE FATHER OF YOTO

SWEET human hearts—a tale of carnival, moon-haunted nights: a tale of the spring-tide, of the flower and the leaf ripening to fruit: a gossamer thing of dreamy-lanterned streets, told by my friend, Tai Ling, of West India Dock Road. Its scene is not the Hoang Ho or the sun-loved islands of the East, but Limehouse. Nevertheless it is a fairy tale, because so human.

Marigold Vassiloff was a glorious girl. The epithet is not mine, but Tai Ling's. Marigold lived under the tremendous glooms of the East and West India Docks; and what she didn't know about the more universal aspects of human life, though she was yet short of twenty, was hardly to be known. You know, perhaps, the East India Dock, which lies a little north of its big brother, the West India Dock: a place of savagely masculine character, evoking the brassy mood. By daytime a cold, nauseous light hangs about it; at night a devilish darkness settles upon it.

You know, perhaps, the fried-fish shops that punctuate every corner in the surrounding maze of streets, the "general" shops with their assorted rags, their broken iron, and their glum-faced basins of kitchen waste; and the lurid-seeming creatures that glide from nowhere into nothing—Arab, Lascar, Pacific Islander, Chinky, Hindoo, and so on, each carrying his own perfume. You know, too, the streets of plunging hoof and horn that cross and recross the waterways, the gaunt chimneys that stick their derisive tongues to the skies. You know the cobbly courts, the bestrewn alleys, through which at night gas-jets asthmatically splutter; and the mephitic glooms and silences of the dockside. You know these things, and I need not attempt to illuminate them for you.

But you do not know that in this place there are creatures with the lust for life racing in their veins; creatures hot for the moment and its carnival; children of delicate graces; young hearts asking only that they may be happy for their hour. You do not know that there are girls on these raw edges of London to whom silks and wine and song are things to be desired but never experienced. Neither do you know that one of these creatures, my Marigold, was the heroine of one of the most fantastic adventures of which I have heard.

It may offend your taste, and in that case you may reject it. Yet I trust you will agree that any young thing, moving in that dank daylight, that devilish darkness, is fully justified in taking her moments of gaiety as and when she may. There may be callow minds that cry No; and for them I have no answer. There are minds to which the repulsive—such as Poplar High Street—is supremely beautiful, and to whom anything frankly human is indelicate, if not ugly. You need, however, to be a futurist to discover ecstatic beauty in the torn wastes of tiles, the groupings of iron and stone, and the nightmare of chimney-stacks and gas-works. Barking Road, as it dips and rises with a sweep as lovely as a flying bird's, may be a thing to fire the trained imagination, and so may be the subtle tones of flame and shade in the byways, and the airy tracery of the Great Eastern Railway arches. But these crazy things touch only those who do not live among them: who comfortably wake and sleep and eat in Hampstead and Streatham. The beauty which neither time nor tears can fade is hardly to be come by east of Aldgate Pump; if you look for it there and think that you find it, I may tell you that you are a *poseur*; you may take your seat at a St. John's Wood breakfast-table, and stay there.

Marigold was not a futurist. She was an apple-cheeked girl, lovely and brave and bright. The Pool at night never shook her to wonder. Masthead, smokestack, creaking crane, and the perfect chiming of the overlying purples evoked nothing responsive in her. If she desired beauty at all, it was the beauty of the chocolate box or the biscuit tin. Wherefore Poplar and Limehouse were a weariness to her. She was a malcontent; and one can hardly blame her, for she was a girl of girls. When she dreamed of happier things, which she did many times a week, and could not get them, she took the next best thing. A sound philosophy, you will agree. She flogged a jaded heart in the loud music hall, the saloons of the dockside, and found some minutes' respite from the eternal grief of things in the arms of any salt-browned man who caught her fancy.

Tai Ling was right. She was a moon-blossom. Impossible to imagine what she might have been in gentler surroundings. As it was she was too cruelly beautiful for human nature's daily food. Her face had not the pure and perfect beauty such as you may find in the well-kept inmates of an Ealing High School. But above that face was a crown of thunderous hair, shot with an elfish sheen, which burned the heart out of any man creature who spotted her. She was small, but ripe-breasted, and moved like a cat. The very lines of her limbs were an ecstasy, and she had, too, an odd, wide laugh—and knew how to use it.

Now it happened one night, when her head was tangled in a net of dreams, that she sought escape in the Causeway, in the little white café where you may take noodle, chop suey, China tea, and other exotic foods.

She was the only white thing there. Yellow men and brown were there, and one tan-skinned woman, but Marigold was the only pure product of these islands. At a far table, behind the bead curtain in the corner, sat Tai Ling. He saw her, and lit to a sudden delight of her.

Tai Ling was a queer bird. Not immoral, for, to be immoral, you must first subscribe to some conventional morality. Tai Ling did not. You cannot do wrong until you have first done right. Tai Ling had not. He was just non-moral; and right and wrong were words he did not understand. He was in love with life, and song, and wine, and warmth, and the beauty of little girls. The world to him, as to Marigold, was a pause on a journey, where one might take one's idle pleasure, while others strewed the path with mirth and roses. He knew only two divisions of people—the gay and the stupid. The problems of this life and the next passed him by. He never turned aside from pleasure, or resisted an invitation to the feast.

In fact, by our standards, a complete rogue; yet the most joyous I have known. I never knew a man with so seductive a smile. It has driven the virtuously indignant heart out of me many a time, and I never knew a girl, white or coloured, who could withstand it. I almost believe it would have beaten down the frigid steel ramparts that begird the English "lady." It thrilled and tickled you as does the gayest music of Mozart. It had not the mere lightness of frivolity, but, like that music, it had the deep-plumbing gaiety of the love of life, for joy and sorrow.

The moment Tai Ling caught Marigold's eye, the heart in him sprang like a bird to song, and he began to smile. I say began, for an Oriental smile is not an affair of a swift moment. It has a birth and a beginning. It awakes—hesitates—grows, and at last from the sad chrysalis emerges the butterfly.

A Chinese smile at the full is one of the subtlest expressions of which the human face is capable.

The mischief was done. Marigold went down before that smile without even putting up her guard. Swift on the uptake, she tossed it back to him, and her maddening laugh ran across the room. Tai Ling waited until she drew out a frowsy packet of cigarettes; then back to her he carried the laugh, and slipped a lighted match over her shoulder almost before the cigarette was at her mouth.

It was aptly done. He sat down beside her, and took graceful charge of her hand, while he encircled her waist. He had been flying to and fro long enough on P. & O. boats to have picked up, during his London sojourns, a fair Cockney vocabulary, which he used with a liquid accent; and he began talk with her, in honey-flavoured phrases, of Swatow, of Yokohama, Fuji Yama, Sarawak; of flowered islands, white towns and green bays, and sunlight like wine, and . . . oh, a thousand things that the little cloudy head spun at hearing.

They had more tea and cigarettes, and he bought a scented spice for her, and they left the café together, at about midnight, very glad.

* * *

When Marigold gave herself to Tai Ling, as I have explained in that row of dots, she did so because she was happy, and because Tai Ling had amused her, and was pleased with her. But why she met him again and yet again, it is difficult to say. It is difficult also to understand why Tai Ling, who so loved sunshine, and flower and blue water, should have lingered in fusty Limehouse for the space of a year. But the two of them seemed to understand their conduct, and both were happy. For Tai Ling had a little apartment in the Causeway, and thither Marigold would flit from time to time, until . . .

One evening, as they loafed together in the hot, lousy dusk, when the silence was so sharp that a footstep seemed to shatter the night, he learnt, in a flood of joy and curiosity and apprehension, that he was about to become papa.

It overwhelmed him. He nearly choked. It was so astounding, so new, so wonderful, so . . . everything that was inexpressible. Such a thing had not happened before to him. Hitherto, he had but loved and ridden away, the gay deceiver. But now——He questioned, and conjectured what was to be done; and Marigold replied airily that it didn't matter much; that if she had a little money she could arrange things. She spoke of a Poplar hospital . . . good treatment . . . quite all right; and thereupon she collapsed at his feet in a tempest of curls and tears.

With that, his emotions cleared and calmed, and resolved themselves into one definite quantity—pride. He drew Marigold on to the cushions, and kissed her, and in his luscious tongue he sang to her; and this is, roughly, what he sang: an old song known to his father:

"O girl, the streams and trees glory in the glamour of spring; the bright sun drops about the green shrubs, and the falling flowers are scattered and fly away. The lonely cloud moves to the hill, and the birds find their leafy haunts. All things have a refuge to which they fly, but I alone have nothing to which to cling. Wherefore, under the moon I drink and sing to the fragrant blossom, and I hold you fast, O flower of the waters, O moon-blossom, O perfect light of day!

"Violets shall lie shining about your neck, and roses in your hair. Your holy hands shall be starred about with gems. Over the green and golden hills, and through the white streets we will wander while the dawn is violet-lidded; and I will hide you in your little nest at night, and love shall be over you for ever!"

That was his song, sung in Chinese. It was old—such songs are not now written in the country of Tai Ling, except by imitators—and Tai Ling might well have forgotten it in the hard labours of his seaman's life. But he had not, and when it was finished, Marigold was pleased, and clung to him, and told him that she so loved him that she must not inflict this trouble upon him. But he would not hear her.

"No-no-no, Malligold," he murmured, while they raptured, "Malligold—lou shall not go. Lou shall stay with Tai Ling. Oh, lou'll have evelything beautiful, all same English lady. Tai Ling have heap money—les—and lou shall have a li'l room. . . . Blimey—les . . . clever doctors . . . les."

And he managed it. He arranged that chamber and that landlady, and that doctor and nurse were duly booked. And he glided in great joy next evening to the café, to inform his friends that he was about to have an heir. He talked loudly and volubly in his rich seaman's lingo, and suddenly, in the same language, a voice shot through the clamour:

"Tai Ling, you speak no truth!"

Tai Ling sprang up, and his hand flew to the waist of his cotton trousers, and flew back, grasping a kreese.

"Tai Ling," repeated the voice, still in Chinese, "I say you lie. *I* am the father of li'l Malligold's babe!"

At that moment, anything might have happened, had not two shirt-sleeved waiters slipped dexterously between the claimants, and grasped their wrists. Tai Ling's face was aflame with as much primitive emotion as an Oriental face may show. But his first rage died, as another voice came from the bead curtain at the rear of the little cluster.

"Tai Ling, Wing Foo, you both speak no truth. For Malligold has told me even this evening that the child is mine!" And the third claimant thrust a vehement face through the curtain, and swam down among them. "I," he cried, his hands quarrelling nervously at his bosom, "I—I am the father of Malligold's man-child!"

The glances of the three met like velveted blades. For one moment tragedy was in the air. Knives were still being grasped.

Then Tai Ling began his conquering smile. It was caught by the crowd and echoed, and in another moment light laughter was running about, with chattering voices and gesturing hands. The waiters released their hold on the prospective fathers, and the three competitors sat down to a table and called for tea and sweet cakes and cigarettes.

One must admit that Marigold's conduct was, as the politicians say, deserving of the highest censure; but, you see, she was young, and she needed money for this business—her first. Some small amounts, it appeared, she had managed to collect from Wing Foo and his friend, but neither of them had done what Tai Ling had done so magnanimously. You would have thought, perhaps, that by all the traditions of his race, Ling would have been exceedingly wroth at this discovery of infidelity on the part of one who had shared his bed. But he was not. He sat at the table, and smiled that inscrutable, shattering smile, and in fancy he folded Marigold within his brown arms. His was an easy-going disposition; human kindliness counted with him before tradition and national beliefs. A sweet fellow. A rogue himself, he did not demand perfection in others. No; the infidelity did not anger him. The only point about the business that really disturbed him was that there should be others who aspired to the fatherhood of this, Marigold's first child, and, he believed, his.

So they sat and talked it over, and when they parted, and each went his way into the night, to tell his tale, Tai Ling went to the Poplar Hippodrome to drown his perplexity. There he witnessed the performance of a Chinese juggler, who blasphemed his assistants in the language of Kennington Gate, and was registered on the voting list at Camberwell as Rab M'Andrew. After sitting in the hall for some hour and a half, his ideas were adjusted, and he went to the house where Marigold was, and gently charged her with what he had heard. She fell at once to tears and protestations and explanations, and desired to go away from him for ever. She had not meant wrong; but . . . she did not know . . . and she had so wanted the money . . . and . . .

Well, he would not let her go. He caught her back, and thrust his forgiveness upon her; and the whole affair ought to have ended in disaster for both of them. But it did not, as you will see.

The next morning, there was a new development. The story of the café conversation was racing about Limehouse and Poplar, when it came to the ears of one, Chuck Lightfoot, a pugilistic promoter. Now parenthood is not an office which the Englishman lightly assumes, but Chuck straightway butted in, and demanded to know, with menaces, what was the matter with his claim. It wasn't that he was specially anxious to father the child. Indeed, the success of his claim, and the resultant financial outlay, would have seriously disconcerted him. It was just the principle of the thing that riled him. Damn it, he wasn't going to stand by and be dished by any lousy scarleteer of a yellow devil; not much. He asserted further that by reference to dates he could prove many things which went far to establish his claim; and, finally, if anyone wanted a fight, they'd only got to ask for it.

Apparently no one did; for Tai Ling went about with that smile of his, and shook all seriousness out of them. During the week he called a convocation at the house where he had installed Marigold, and where she now lay, and there they gathered—three yellow men, proud, jealous, reticent, and one vehement white man, hot-eared, inarticulate, and still ready to fight the lot of 'em. Clearly a mistake had happened somewhere. There had obviously been a miscalculation on somebody's part, to say nothing of a regrettable oversight. But whose child it was remained for proof.

There, then, Marigold lay in a comfortable bed, comfortably attended, awaiting her time; while four men, only politely recognising each other's existence, sat below and wrangled for the honour of the fatherhood. Was ever a woman in so shameful and so delicious a situation?

At about four o'clock on Saturday afternoon, it happened. . . .

News was brought downstairs. The child was yellow-white, with almond eyes, and it was unmistakably the child of Tai Ling.

Three of the claimants faded away before Tai Ling's sweet obeisances and compliments, like wind over the grass; the third went raucously, with fierce gesture and trivial abuse.

Now in Tai Ling's heart was great joy, and he ambled about that house, in his sleek little way, doing delicate, pretty things which no white man could have done or conceived. Seldom has a wooing and matrimony, so conducted, led to the house of bliss. But that is where Marigold and Tai Ling are living.

One day, when the baby Yoto was six weeks old, there arrived at the house six clusters of white flowers and six scented boxes—one for Marigold, one for Yoto, and one each for the three disappointed claimants; and, these love-gifts were duly delivered by Tai Ling himself to the recipients, all of whom received them sweetly, save Chuck Lightfoot; and what he said or did is of no account.

Tai Ling and Marigold are still in West India Dock Road, and very prosperous and happy they are, though, as I say, they have no right to be.

Yoto has now a brother and a sister, each of whom is the owner of a little scented box. Visit them all one day, at the provision shop, which is the third as you pass Pennyfields; and they will tell you this story more delicately and fragrantly than I.

GRACIE GOODNIGHT

GRACIE GOODNIGHT had the loveliest hair that ever was seen east of Aldgate Pump—where lies that land of lovely girls and luxurious locks. It was this head of hers—melodious as an autumn sunset—that turned the discordant head of old fat Kang Foo Ah, and made it reel with delicious fancies, and led him to hire her as a daily girl to clean up his home and serve in his odoriferous shop.

It was legendary in Limehouse that old Kang Foo Ah knew a thing or three. When he took that little shop in Pennyfields, business was, according to those best qualified to speak, rotten. Yet now—in the short space of eighteen months—he had a very comfortable fortune stowed away in safe places known to himself. Where his predecessor and his rivals laid out threepence and made fourpence, Kang Foo Ah would lay out threepence and make sixpence-halfpenny. As he stood behind his counter, with the glorious-headed Gracie, nimble-fingered and deft of brain, at his side, he would smile blandly upon her and upon his customers; his hands, begemmed like a Hatton Garden Jew's, folded across his stomach. He positively exuded prosperity, so that its waves seemed to beat upon you and set you tingling with that veneration which the very wisest of us feel toward material success.

Everything of the best and latest was in his shop. There were dried sharks' fins, pickled eggs, twenty years old, bitter melons, lychee fruits, dried chrysanthemum buds, tea, sweet cakes, "chandu" and its apparatus, betel nut, some bright keen knives, and an automatic cash register; while on the walls were Chinese prints, *The Police Budget*, strips of dried duck and fish, some culinary utensils, and three little black bottles of fire-extinguisher, with printed instructions for use, which showed that Kang Foo Ah was doing so well that he had insured his premises with a respectable fire insurance company.

Oh—and, of course, there was Gracie Goodnight; perhaps the happiest touch which earned for Kang's store the reputation of having always the best and the latest. The boys, yellow and white and black, would come to the store and spend more money than they could afford on cigarettes which they didn't want and dried fruits which they couldn't eat; and Gracie would throw out casual invitations to come again and bring a friend and have a cup of tea in the little curtained room at the back, where she served or sat in converse of an evening.

So they came again, and the bank balance of Kang Foo Ah . . . did it not grow and flourish exceedingly, like the green bay-tree? It did; and as he grew fatter and more prosperous, so, like all mankind, he grew more independent, insolent, overbearing. In a current phrase, he began to throw himself about. In another current phrase, equally expressive, though less polite, he began to make himself a damned nuisance. At times he was simply unbearable; yet there was none in Chinatown to stand up to him and put him back in his place. They endured him meekly, because he was successful and they were not.

The honour of putting him to bed was reserved for an insignificant gentleman, not of Chinatown, who resided on the borders of Poplar and Blackwall. He kept the Blue Lantern, at the corner of Shan-tung Place, and it was a respectable house; he had often said so. Now as Kang Foo Ah had never yet known any to stand up to him, he foolishly began to believe that none ever would do so. He overlooked the fact that he had never yet matched himself against the landlord of a London public-house. . . .

This story properly begins with Kang tumbling into the private bar of the aforesaid house, and demanding a gin and rum, mixed. The landlord declined to serve him. Kang called him pseudonyms.

Then the landlord spoke, wagging an illustrative finger as one who makes the Thirdly point in his Advent sermon.

"Look here," he said, "I don't mind you coming to my 'ouse and getting drunk. No. *But* . . . what I do object to is yer getting drunk at someone else's 'ouse, and coming 'ere to be sick. Now clear out, old cock, and toddle 'ome. A lemon-and-bismuth, and you'll be top-hole in the morning. Off yeh go."

Kang caught the bar with both hands, and leered in his slimy way.

"Kang Foo Ah fine fellow . . ." he began; but he was cut short.

"Listen," said Boniface. "Shall I tell you what you are? Yer a perfect dam nuisance to any decent 'ouse. That's what you are. A perfect dam nuisance. Yeh never come 'ere but what yer drunk. Never. Yeh may be a very clever chap, and yeh may have lots of money. But yer a damned nuisance, and it won't trouble me if I never see yer fat face in my 'ouse again. And that's telling yeh. Straight. Yeh know now, doncher? Now beat it, else I'll sick the cops on yeh. Beat it."

In the phrase in which the only onlooker told the story, Kang was properly told off. He slithered and gibbered for a moment; then he was propelled by the shoulder, through the swing doors, to the cold pavement beyond. His voice could be heard in protest.

"Fairly got the monkeys," said the landlord to the only onlooker, as he returned to the bar. "Fairly got 'em. 'Ear what he called me?"

"Got the monkeys?" echoed the only onlooker, who had never forgotten that he had once been refused credit by this house. "I should think 'e would get the monkeys. Anyone'd git the monkeys wiv you talkin' to 'em like that. Got no tack, you ain't. Bin and lorst a good customer, now, and all because of yer swank. Didn' you tell 'im you'd be glad to miss 'is vacant face? Didn' you say 'e was the stink what comes out of Wapping at night? Didn' you say 'e'd make a bug sorry 'e was masheeshing around in the same bed with 'im? Course 'e got the monkeys. Who wouldn't? You oughter learn tack."

Yes; Kang Foo Ah had got the monkeys. He had them so badly that when he returned to the shop in Pennyfields, and caught Gracie in the act of nicking a few dry cakes, he discharged her. He did not discharge her with any great exercise of "tack." He merely bellowed upon her to go; and when she stood looking at him in dumb wonder, he grabbed her by the shoulders, pinched her neck, tore at her lovely hair, and thrust her bodily over the step into the narrow street, even as himself had been flung by the keeper of the Blue Lantern. He tossed her hat and jacket after her, crying:

"Go, thieving girl! Go, robber. Daughter of a dog . . . Go!"

Now in, Gracie's heart there burned a very savage flame of self-respect. She was fond of herself, and her trim little person and her wondrous hair were to her sacred things, not lightly to be mauled by anyone, and certainly to be held pure from the loathly yellow hands of a Chinky. But what fed that flame with furious fuel was Kang's roared accusation of *Thief.* All Pennyfields—Chinks and whites—turned out to hear and to see. They cackled and chi-iked. All heard the wretched name. Many saw the violent expulsion, and latecomers arrived at least in time for the fun of seeing Gracie retrieve her hat and jacket from the puddle where they had fallen, put them on, and march away crying frightful things upon her employer, and throwing, deftly, a piece of road mud so that it spread, pancake-wise, over his window. None moved to help her or to sympathise; they were either telling or hearing the tale; and, beautiful as she might be, she was now a figure for ridicule, a thing of no account, cast down and unheroic. They had patronised the shop for her smiles and her chatter; but now she was absurd, and her physical charms availed her nothing in this moment of undignified distress. They stood around and laughed. They pointed fingers, and their mouths went wide at the pathetic, screaming, stamping little figure, whose flying hair, ruffled clothing, vociferant hands and impotent indignation gave her momentarily the air of a pantomime dame.

"I'll git back on him. Christ, I will!" she cried, and kicked a furious foot in his direction as she swept like a baby tornado into West India Dock Road. She'd fix him, good and plenty. She'd learn him to fire white girls out like that. She'd learn him to put his slimy hands on her neck, and to mess his fingers in Gracie Goodnight's hair. She'd show him what. You wait. Not today, perhaps, or tomorrow, but she'd get him all right, before long. She'd put it acrost him for calling Gracie Goodnight a thief. She'd show the nasty, dirty, slimy, crawling, leery old reptile how he could catch hold of a decent girl with his beastly, filthy, stinking, yellow old fingers. Not half, she wouldn't. . . .

Of course, she had stolen. Admitted at once. But would anyone but that fat old beast take any notice of a mouldy old cake? And then to sling you off without notice. And in that way, too—putting his hands on you and throwing you out. And then chucking your things at you in the gutter. Oh, my word . . . but he'd cop out.

He did. . . .

Gracie cried herself to sleep on her solitary and doubtfully clean pillow that night, after much hard thinking. Two days later, after a consultation with a few pals at a near corner, she came to the loud conclusion that pride was all very well, and all that sort of thing; but after all, you'd got to live somehow. She would, then, sink her pride, and go and ask old fat Kang Foo Ah to take her back and give her another chance. It was known that the two days had marked a distinct drop in the takings of the store, especially in the little curtained room at the back where tea and cakes were served of an evening. Probably he'd be glad to overlook it, and take her on again. She would go that night; and she let all Chinatown know of her decision to ask pardon of Kang.

That night she went. It was a reasonably clear night, for Limehouse, and the lights of the Asiatic quarter glowed like bright beads against their mellow backgrounds of ebony and olive. A sharp breeze from the river rushed up Pennyfields, and shop signs were swaying, and skirts and petticoats were being blown about, teasing the yellow boys with little peeps of delicate stocking and soft leg. Gracie came along with her friends, holding hats and bowing before the wind. She had brought her friends because, she said, she felt rather kind of squiffy about the job, and it would sort of buck her up if they went with her. Besides, you never knew: he might fly at her again.

The expected happened, as it usually does. Kang Foo Ah was again in a bad mood. He was seated behind his counter, gazing ruefully at the little tearoom, now empty of voice and light laughter and revenue. A large white-shaded lamp stood firmly on the counter, and, for the rest, the shop was lighted by two Chinese lanterns which hung dreamily on the wall.

To him went Gracie, bold of bearing but knocking at the knees. Outside, in the narrow roadway, her three friends—two girls and a lad—stood to watch the fun and, if need be, to render assistance. They saw Gracie go in and address her master. They saw him start up and wag a severe head. They saw Gracie press the argument, and move to the side of the counter against the lamp. Words passed. The old man seemed to grow angry; his gestures and his lips were far from friendly. Gracie leaned forward with a new argument. His face darkened, He answered. Gracie retorted. Then his great arm shot swiftly up. Gracie jumped back with the fleetness of a startled faun. Her muff caught the white china lamp. It went with a crash and a rush of flame to the floor.

The oil ran, and the fire flew up to the counter where the dried skins hung. In five seconds the shop window was ablaze. Gracie screamed. The old man roared; and they both screamed again, for, in jumping backward, Gracie had struck with the feather of her hat one of the pendulous lanterns which, thus agitated, had fired itself, and the flaming paper had dropped on Kang's side of the counter, where were candles and an oil-tank.

Pennyfields, through the voices of Gracie's three friends, screamed too, and swiftly the shops and the lodging-houses were cleared of their companies. Over pavement and roadway the yellow boys crowded and danced and peered, while Gracie stood still, her hands at her glorious head, screaming . . . screaming . . . screaming. . . .

The massive dignified Kang Foo Ah roared and capered, for he was imprisoned in the narrow space behind the counter, and fire was all about him. The doorway was blocked with mad flames; exit was impossible there; and the oil-tank at the other end shot random spears in every direction. Gracie, with crouching limbs and hands clasped in a gesture of primitive fear, crept back and back. They were lovely hands, white and slim and shapely, and even as he danced and howled, Kang wondered why he had driven them away from his counter. The boy friend outside made a gallant effort to dash in to her, but smoke and flame easily beat him off.

Now the street began to scream useless advice, admonition and encouragement. Women in safety added their little bit to the screaming. They cried that it would spread, and soon furniture from distant houses was crashing and bounding to the pavement; and mattresses were flung out from upper windows, to receive the indecent figures of their owners. Above the clamour a lone voice cried something intelligible, and soon one heard an engine that raved and jangled in West India Dock Road.

Kang Foo Ah danced to the rhythm of a merry tune. "Save me! Save me!" he babbled. "I give heap plenty money anyone save me. I give hundred pounds—two hundred pounds—anyone save me. Ooo! Save me!" And his voice trailed into mournful nothings.

But Gracie had now crept back to the little tearoom, and she cried, in her clear, shrill voice: "Stand still, mister! I'll save you. I'm going to save you!" And, to the crowd: "Stand clear, there! I know a way to save him. Mind the glass! Look out!"

A swift white hand reached to the wall and dragged down the little wire cage holding the extinguisher bottles which the wary insurance company had provided. But when Kang saw what she would be at, he danced a dervish dance more furiously, and roared at her in great agony.

"No—no—no. Get water. Get water. Ao! Put bottles down. *Ao!*"

But in the oblivious courage of the desperate, Gracie heard him not. She held one bottle poised in a light hand, approached as near the flames as she dared, and flung it shrewdly and accurately at his feet. The second she flung, and the third she flung, and then dropped back, panting from the heat and the smoke, to the tearoom, where she clutched with fumbling fingers at the bead curtain, and collapsed in a swoon.

And terrible things now happened. For the first bottle and the second bottle and the third bottle smashed at the feet of Kang Foo Ah, and the fire did not subside. It rose over the counter, faster and faster, until he was swallowed in a mouth of white fire, through which, for a moment, one saw his idiot yellow face and antic limbs. Then, mercifully, he disappeared. . . .

The engine, brave with noise and glitter, forced a way up the street, and in ten minutes the men had the fire well under, and Gracie was on the pavement with first-aid men about her. As the water coursed over her neck, and the brandy slid between her lips, she made little movements, and murmured.

"I done my best," she sobbed. "I done my best. I tried to save him. And the shop, too. What happened? Is he all right?"

"Now, kid," said the crowd, "that's all right. Don't you worry. Feeling better? That's the style."

"Yes; you done all right, you did. No; we couldn't get him. He was under before we could get in. Extinguishers wasn't much good in that bloody furnace."

"It was the damn pluckiest thing ever I see. You done your best. No one can't do more'n that. Way you kept your nerve and copped hold of them things."

"I see it all, I did. 'Aving a row, wasn't you? When he knocked the lamp over, trying to wollop you one? Ah, he was an old blighter, when all's said and done."

So Gracie, pale, trembling and dumb, was lifted to her feet and handed over to her friends, who took her home. The inquest was held next day, and various witnesses were called, including the three friends who had seen everything from start to finish. And Gracie was complimented by the Coroner and the Brigade Superintendent on her courage, self-control and resource. It was added that the Royal Humane Society had been apprised of the facts of the case; and although Kang Foo Ah had perished in the fire, it was certainly not because anything that could have been done had been left undone; Miss Gracie Goodnight had done more, far more, than anyone, especially a woman, could have been expected to do in such circumstances.

There were cheers for Gracie as she left the court, and four photographers from news agencies and picture papers stepped forward with levelled cameras to get lasting records of that glorious, smiling head. The smile in those pictures, which you may find if you hunt up the files, is as strange and inscrutable as the smile of Mona Lisa, though there is that in its pose which seems to say: "Hands off. I'll learn anybody to mess my hair about."

For, now that Kang Foo Ah is out of it, little Gracie Goodnight is the only person in the world who knows that those extinguisher bottles had been emptied of their contents and refilled with kerosene.

THE PAW

IT was the maidenly month of April, though it was not to be known in Pennyfields except by the calendar: a season of song and quickening blood. Beyond London, amid the spray of meadow and orchard, bird and bee were making carnival, but here one still gambled and waited to find a boat. Limehouse has no seasons. It has not even the divisions of day and night. Boats must sail at all hours at the will of the tide, and their swarthy crews are ever about. It has no means of marking the pomp of the year's procession. Lusty spring may rustle in the hedgerows; golden-tasselled summer may move on the meadows. In Limehouse there are only more seamen or less seamen. Summer is a spell of stickiness, and winter a time of fog. There may perhaps be those who long to escape from it when the calendar calls spring, to kiss their faces to the grass, to lose their tired souls in tangles of green shade; but they are hardly to be met with. For the most, Limehouse is sufficient. These rather futile green fields and songs of birds and bud-spangled trees are all very well, if you have the limited mind, but how much sweeter are the things of the hands, the darling friendliness of the streets!

It was this season of flower and awakening that was the setting for the most shuddering tale that the Chinese quarter can tell.

It is of Greaser Flanagan, gateman at a docks station, and his woman: how she was stolen from him by Phung-tsin, the Chink, and of Flanagan's revenge.

Now Greaser Flanagan was a weak man, physically and morally flabby. Your strong man fears nothing but himself. The Greaser feared everything but himself. He feared God, he feared the devil, and other men's opinions and their hands, and he feared life and death. He did not fear himself, for he was in the wretched position of knowing himself for the thing he was.

He was not a bad man. He had neither the courage for evil nor the tenderness for good. He was a Nothing. He did not smoke. He seldom swore. He did not drink. But he was a bit of a hop-head, and did sometimes hire an upper room in the Causeway, and sprawl his restless nerves on the solitary bed, with a pipe of *li-un* or a handful of snow, and from it snatch some of the rich delights that life gave to others.

Now narcotised sensibilities are all very well for the grey routine of life. They help you to bridge the gaps. They carry you through the tedium of things, and hold you in velvet and silk against the petty jolts and jars.

But when the big crisis comes, the grief of a lifetime . . . well, that you feel just ten times deeper and longer than the normal person. God! How it bites and stings and lacerates, and bites again, and tears the roots out of you, and creeps into every nerve and tissue of you, and sucks at the bones! How it scalds and itches and bruises and burns the body of you, and colours every moment of thought, and strangles your sleep!

So the Greaser found it. For the Greaser loved his wife with the miserable, furious passion of a weak thing. He loved her to life and death as such men do when they rise to it at all. He only lived when with her. Opium could not give him what even the sense of neighbourhood with her could give him. Of all things in the world he loved only her; his crawling blood only ran warm when she was by.

Which was not as often as it should have been, for she took her departures when and as she chose. Sometimes she would be out for a day, and return in the dark morning, without explanation or excuse.

And suddenly, on a bright Sunday, he lost her for all. She went from him to a yellow man in Pennyfields, leaving a derisive note of final farewell. The brutality of the blow got him like a knife on a wound. Something fouled within him, and for an hour or so he was stupid—a mere flabby Thing in a cotton suit. Then, as his faculties returned, they returned in fevered form. Something had happened. He was a new man—a man with an idea—a fixed goal—a haunting.

The Chinky must be killed. He wanted to kill him, but he knew he had not the pluck or the strength to do it. Did he hate Daffodil, his girl? No; he loved her with a more absurd little passion than before. He wanted her back, but not to harm her. It was the Chinky on whom all his thin rage was directed.

The Chinky must be killed. The Chinky must be killed.

Round and round his brain it rolled. . . . Kill the Chink. He realised dimly that his life had now but one purpose, the outing of the Chink. In his slow, untaught mind a dozen snakely schemes uncoiled themselves, but all were impracticable for him. For all his brute ignorance, however, he had, as people of the soil often have, a perception which sometimes leads directly to surprisingly shrewd conclusions, to which the educated mind only comes by steps of thought.

He sat on the edge of a rickety chair, his hands on his knees, his face to the floor; and so he sat, all through that Sunday evening, thinking, planning; now determined, now fearing. But that night he began his work, and in five days it was done.

There had been born to Daffodil and the Greaser a daughter. He had never much noticed the child, for he was not demonstrative, and was not at ease with any children or animals. The three of them had lived in one dirty, bare room in the throttled byway of Formosa Terrace, one room in which they commonly lived, slept, ate and toileted. As he lay on his ragged bed, sleepless, that night, he suddenly saw, clearly, as though the Fates had placed it in his hand, the weapon whereby he should achieve his desire. He dared not do it himself. His limbs had shaken for hours at the mere notion of the act. He was afraid of a fight with the Chinky; and he leapt to a cold, wet terror at the prospect of the Old Bailey and the light cord. But . . . as this new idea came to him, he lay and shivered with joy; the joy that a craftsman will take in a difficult task skilfully performed. In fifteen minutes it was all planned. It could be done—oh, easy! The result would hurt no one. A few years' detention in a good home for the culprit, and then release under official auspices—nothing of any consequence. He knew well the material he had to work upon—nervous, resilient material, responsive to suggestion, half paralysed by command—and how to work upon it in such a way that nothing could be traced to him. Oh, it was too damned easy, with that material—namely, the fruit of a hysterical, erotic girl and a weedy opium-jolter. He lay and pinched his white face and the limp hair about his mouth, and chortled. He would start now. In the corner of the room farthest from the window was young Myrtle's mattress. He crawled out of bed, stretched himself horribly, and moved over the bare floor to where she lay lost and lovely in sleep. Had the Greaser heard of what he was about to do as the conduct of another, he would have turned sick. But the man was mad, soberly mad. The thought of having the horrid Chinky stark and stiff and bloodless in a day or two was so sweet that it burned all other emotion out of him. Gawd—to think of it! Even now, when Limehouse Church was squeaking one o'clock, perhaps the Chinky's lemon hands were upon the skin of his Daffodil! Now, perhaps, he was stripping her, kissing, with his long, wet lips, all the beauty of white arms and breast, and knowing by now, as well as the Greaser, every bit of that shining body that had been his for eleven years, and still was his—his—his! Gawd! It was suffocating to think about! If he was a strong man—if he could get the throat of the lousy Chinky in his hands, and squeeze the wind out of it! But he had seen him fight, he knew the dexterity of his tactics. That dexterity, however, would not avail against this new scheme.

So he grabbed the thin blanket that covered Myrtle, flung it off, and, before she was awake, half-a-dozen sharp, light blows had fallen on the exposed little form from a switch. Three gasps of surprise, and then a scream of pain tore through the night. Again and again he whipped her, against her screams and struggles. All about the writhing limbs the fang fell, until screams and appeals sank to moans and a fight for breath; and then a hoarse voice came to her out of the dark:

"Know what that's for?" She had not the strength to force a word, but at a sharp cut she pleaded through automatic sobs.

"That's 'cos yer ma's gone with the yeller man, that is. So now yer know. The yeller man took yer ma away, damn 'im, and I gotter look after yeh meself now. So that'll learn yeh to be'ave yerself—see? Someone ought to stick a knife into that bloody Chink—that's what they ought. Now, hold yer row and go to sleep, else you'll have some more."

As quickly as he had descended on her, he left her and returned to bed, and there he lay murmuring to himself. And when Myrtle, with stifled cries and sobs and chokings, fell at last into a late sleep, it was with terror in her heart, and a voice in her ears that was mumbling: "Someone's gotter stick a knife inside that bloody Chink!"

Next morning he said nothing of the happenings of the night, but he did not go to work. And suddenly he called her to him, and stood her between his knees, and so held her in a vice. For some three minutes he held her thus, staring at her, silent and motionless. The child stood, scarcely supported by the little strength that was in her, like a mesmerised rabbit.

Then a hand concealed behind him shot up savagely at her cheek. She reeled, but made no movement to break away, and as she fell sideways across him, a lean dog-whip curled with a clever crack about her legs. He made her stand up, and caressed her with the whip, letting her cower away, and bringing her smartly back, and then, through her strangled screams and moans, she became aware that he was singing. The tune was a music-hall lilt, and the song was:

"Someone oughter stick a knife—stick a knife—stick a knife—someone oughter stick a knife acrost that bloody Chink!"

On went the merry song, while little supplications, and moans rising to screams, and screams dropping to moans, punctuated it, and with each scream and gasp he suffered a thrill of ecstasy. Then he made her undress, and slashed her round the room, slashed her to a faint, and himself to a whirlwind of profanity, all to the little tune of the Chink. As she dropped in a grey swoon at the window, her eyes closed, her breathing scarcely perceptible, he got the water-jug and flung its contents full over her. A mechanical panting and muscular jerks were the only sign of life; she was now but a quivering organism. But he took her arm and twisted it, and the new shock of pain aroused her to the tune of "Stick a knife—stick a knife—inside that bloody Chink!" She was too weak to make any sound, or to plead for release; and while the Greaser got some cheap whisky from a cupboard, and forced her mouth open, and poured some few drops down, there was a terrible silence where a moment ago had been lunatic screams and the voice of the whip.

Then he dragged her up, and bade her dress, and amused himself with playing the switch about her beaten limbs, still chanting his song; and at last he flung her to a corner, and went out, locking the door upon her.

He had begun his work well. For as she lay there, sick with pain, bleeding and lacerated and quivering, knowing nothing of the reason for this change in the nature of things, but conscious only that it was not so before ma went away, she had in her head a horrible tune that jangled, and would not leave her. It tripped to the racing of her burning pulse, to the throbbing of her scorched body, and to the beating of the dynamo in the gas-station beyond the window:

"Someone ought to stick a knife—stick a knife—stick a knife—someone ought to stick a knife across that bloody Chink!"

What happened during the next four days in that loathly room can hardly be told. Day and night there were screamings and entreaties. Not one night's rest did she know. Sleep for an hour he would give her, and then she would be awakened by a voice singing a familiar song of "Stick-a-knife," and lean hands that worked horrors upon her rosy limbs.

The lemon-coloured curls and the delicate, light beauty of her, so like her mother, must often have smote him, but he never swerved from his aim, and in a day or two she became an automaton, anticipating his wish, moving at a turn of his head, obedient to his unspoken word. As his idea progressed by these methods he found that the beast that lies in all of us had burst its chain, and a lust of torture possessed him. He seemed to lose himself in a welter of cruelty, yet never lost his sense of direction.

In the intervals of these debauches and the pursuance of his plan, his love-mad heart would be full to sickness for his lost Daffodil, and the beauty of her, and her ways and speech—how thus she would go, and thus, and say so and so. He would awake at night and not find her by him, and his very bones would yearn for the girl who had chucked him for a yellow man. And then he would think upon his plan, and, thinking upon that, he would try to further it; and once the beast of cruelty was loosed again, it would run in him with a consuming pace, until he began to fear that the child would be too overdone for his desire.

At last, on the fourth day, he neared the end. She had been laid across the chair and beaten almost to physical insensibility, and the inevitable reaction on the mind had left her mentally quiescent, blank. He had timed it cunningly. For all his abandonment to the passion of torment, some poison in his blood had led him clearly to his goal; and it was almost with a shriek of glee that he heard her speak after one of those assaults which she had come to regard as normal and to accept without surprise.

"Dad—why don't someone kill the Chink, then?"

He held himself well in hand, and answered casually: "'Cos they're all afraid, that's why."

"No one couldn't kill the Chink, could they?"

"Course they could. Easy. Any afternoon. All them lot goes to sleep every afternoon—Chinky, too, in a dark room. Anyone could kill 'im then. As easy! I'd like someone to do it, that I would. Taking yer ma away from you and me, dammim!"

"How'd they do it, then?"

"Why——" He caught her by the frock, and dragged her to him. The physical pain of the four days had left her half animal, and in her face, swollen with tears, was a vacant look with less of intelligent consciousness than a cat's. She did not notice that the hand that pulled her was not cruel, but gentle. "Why, easy he'd do it. He'd go to the Chink's house—the brown 'un at the corner—and he'd slip through the door, 'cos it's alwis open. And he'd creep to the back room where the Chinky sleeps, all in the dark. And he'd creeeeep up to the bed. And he'd have the knife in both hands. And he'd bring it down—Squelch!—into the Chinky's neck—so!"

He pantomimed, and noticed with delight that the child's face was drawn, as in one who strives to learn a lesson.

"But why don' someone do it, then, and bring ma back to us?"

"Oh—'cos they're afraid. And 'cos they mustn't—that's why. It'd be murder. Killing people ain't right. Murder's awful wicked."

"Don't you wish Chinky was dead, dad? I do."

"Not 'arf I don't. I'd be a better man if Chinky was dead. It ain't right to say that, but I wish he was. But there . . . you don't want to think about that kind of thing. It ain't nice. Don't you go thinking about it. And don't talk about it no more. Else you'll get some more of what I just done to yer!"

Next morning, he summoned her, and tore the frock from her, and whipped her again, and tied her to the bed, suspended, so that her feet twisted and just touched the ground. And there he left her till noon. Again and again her aching head would droop, and throw the weight on her arms, and every time she raised it she would see, on the mantelshelf before her, a knife that was not there before—a large, lean knife—and a cheap "sticky-back" photograph—a portrait of the Chink. And as she swayed with the sustained torture, in her little brain sluggish thoughts began to crawl, and the golden head was moved to much strange reasoning.

At noon, he returned and released her, and let her dress, and gave her food. At about three o'clock he departed suddenly, leaving the door unlocked. He stayed away for part of an hour.

When he came back, the room was empty, and he had great joy. His heart sang; he flicked his fingers.

He squatted down by the fetid bed, chewing a piece of betel nut, and waited for her.

At four o'clock he heard the chatter of small feet in the passage, and then a little storm of frock and dishevelled stockings burst into the room, slipped and fell, and rose again, and fell yet again on seeing the Greaser's sensual grin. Her face was whipped to a flame, and her breathing was hard. Her hands clutched the breast of her frock.

"Oh!" was the cry she gave, and for a moment she stood transfixed, expectant of an assault. And when it did not come, she ran on:

"Oh, dad, don't beat me, don't whip me. Daddy, I only run out just to—to do somethink. I done it, dad. I done what they was frightened to do. Dad, aincher glad? I bin and killed him. I bin and killed the Chinky. I done him in, dad. All in the dark. He's dead all right. I put it right in ... both hands. Don't whip me no more. I thought it'd bring ma back, p'r'aps. I thought. ... Oooh! Don't look like that ... dad! ..."

His heart leapt. He could have howled with laughter. He wanted to kick his legs on the bed, and roll about. But he veiled all truth, and stared at the child with a face that assumed a grey terror.

"You done ... what?" he asked, in slow tones of wonder. "You done ... you killed someone. ... Myrtle ... killed that Chink. Oh—my—Gawd!"

"Yes," she said, with stark simplicity, stupidly fingering a large knife which she had drawn from under her frock. "Yep. I done 'im proper. 'Cos he took ma away from us. Look—here's the knife. I went right in, all in the dark. Mind—it's wet. It went right in. It didn't half spurt out."

"Oh, Gawd," he screamed, acting better than he knew. "Blood. Oh, Gawd!" He sank limply to the bed, his figure a question mark. Then he leapt up, dashed to the door, and rushed, in a cloud of words, to the street, crying hoarsely:

"Oh, Gawd! Police! Police! Someone tell the police. My kid's done a murder. Our Myrtle's bin and killed a Chink. Oh, Gawd. Oh, Gawd. Come in, someone. Someone go in to her. She's stuck a knife in a Chink, and she's playing with it, and it's got blood on it. Oh, Gawd, can't someone tell the police!"

In the space of a minute, Formosa Terrace, at that hour torpid and deserted, awoke to furious life. A small, vivid crowd surrounded him, and he stood at its centre, gesturing wildly, his hair dropping, his face working, as, fifty times, he told his tale.

Then a whistle was blown, and slowly the police came; and some went to Pennyfields, to the house of the Chink, and another took the child, and the sergeant took the Greaser and questioned him. He had it all so pat, and was so suitably garrulous and agitated, that he noted with glee how suspicion fell from him.

Yes, the knife was his; it had been given him at the docks by a Malay. Yes, he did hate the Chink because the Chink had taken his wife, the child's mother; and quite probably he had said that the Chink ought to die. Not the right thing to say, perhaps, but quite likely he'd said it, because he felt like that then. No, he hadn't been to work today, but he'd been round at old Benny's most of the morning, and the people downstairs saw him come in about an hour ago. Yes, he had punished the child several times lately. Had had to. His missus had gone with the Chink, and left him alone with the child to look after as well as himself, and he couldn't manage her. He'd had to whip her because she was dirty. (He brushed away a well-forced tear.) But if ever he'd have thought anything like this was going to happen, he'd never have left that knife there. Gawd help him if he would. To think that his kid—his only kid—should do a murder. It was awful. What'd he done to deserve two blows like that? His wife gone; and now his little kid to kill someone. . . . Gawd.

And he broke upon the arms of the supporting constables.

Myrtle and he were taken to the station, the child wondering and a little pleased with the novelty; he with his life's work done, his Daffodil's ravisher put to sleep. His statement was taken again, and he was told that he must consider himself detained with the child, to which he brokenly concurred.

Now there came to the station the officers who had visited the Chink's house, and they made a verbal report of what they had seen.

And suddenly, there burst upon the quiet station a great howl—the howl of a trapped beast, as Greaser Flanagan fell forward over the desk and hammered the floor with his fists.

"Yerss," the constable was saying; "yerss—we bin there. Found the body all right. In bed. Knife wound through the neck—left side. On'y it ain't the Chink. It's a woman. It's Daffodil Flanagan!"

THE CUE

DOWN Wapping way, where the streets rush right and left to waterside and depot, life ran high. Tide was at flood, and below the Old Stairs the waters lashed themselves to fury. Against the savage purple of the night rose a few wisps of rigging and some gruff funnels: lyrics in steel and iron, their leaping lines as correct and ecstatic as a rhymed verse. Under the cold glare of the arc lights, gangs of Asiatics hurried with that impassive swiftness which gives no impression of haste. The acrid tang of the East hung on every breath of air.

Hardly the place to which one would turn as to the city of his dreams; yet there are those who do. Hearts are broken by Blackwall Gardens. The pity and terror and wonder of first love burn in the blood and limbs of those who serve behind the counters of East India Dock Road or load up cargo boats at the landing-stages. Love-mad hands have buried knives in little white bosoms in Commercial Road, and songs are written by the moon across many a happy garret-window in Cable Street.

Once, in these streets, when the gas lamps glimmered and the night was stung with stars, I heard a tale.

*   *   *

The little music hall near the waterside had just slammed its doors on the last stage hand, and stood silent and dark. Stripped of its lights and noise, it gave rather the impression of last night's beer: something flat and stale and squalid. It seemed conscious of the impression it created; there was something shamefaced about it, as of one caught doing unmentionable but necessary things.

At the mouth of the stage-door passage, illumined by a gas jet which flung a light so furtive as to hint that it could show a great deal more if it would, stood a man and a girl. The girl was covered from neck to foot in an old raincoat. The man wore soiled evening-dress, covered by an ulster. A bowler hat rode cockily on one side of his head. A thin cigar thrust itself impetuously from a corner of his large mouth. Approached from behind, he looked English, but his face was flat, and his head was round. The colour of his skin was a murky yellow. He had almonds for eyes. His hair was oily. He was a half-caste: the son of a Shadwell mother and a Chinese father.

He put both hands on the girl's shoulders. He spoke to her, and his face lit with slow passion. She shook her head. She laughed.

"Nit, Chinky, nit. You're a nice old boy, I know, and it was real kind of you to give me all those nice things. But it wouldn't be fair for me to lead you on, y'know. I don't love you. Not a bit. Never did. I've got my boy. The boy I work with. Been with him for five years now, I have. So that's that. And now I must pop off, else the old thing will be wondering what's happened to me."

The half-caste musician glared down at her. He pawed her. He told her, in his labial enunciation, that she was too pretty for music-hall work. He told her that she was a wonderful girl, and murmured: "Sweet, lovely li'l girl. Oh, my beautiful, my beautiful!"

She tittered; and when she moved away he walked by her side, stroking her sleeve. She began to talk conversationally:

"Never mind, old boy. Cheer up. Rotten house tonight, wasn't it? I thought we was going to get the bird, specially when you missed the cue for our change. Oh, and by the way, be careful of those changes, old boy. Y'see, Johnnie's been doing that collapsing trapeze stunt for about five years now, and he always does it to *The Bridal Chorus* music. You want to watch that, y'know; you changed about half-a-tick too soon tonight, and anything like that jars him. See? Well, here's my turning. So long, kid."

But he did not let her go. His tone of casual compliment swiftly changed. He caught her wrists and held them. "I want you!" His straight, flat lips were moist. She drew away; he pulled her to him, bent, swung her from her feet, and crushed her small body against his, bruising her little mouth with angry kisses.

But she raised a sharp hand and pushed him in the face.

"Here—steady on, Chinky!" she cried, using the name which she knew would sting him to the soul. She was disconcerted and inclined to be cross, while half laughing. "Don't take liberties, my son. Specially with me. You're only a yellow rat, y'know."

Something flickered for an instant beneath his long, narrow lashes, and in another instant was gone. He bent again. "O li'l lovely girl. . . . My dear!" Some beast seemed to leap within him. His hands mauled her with intent cruelty, as though he would break and devour her.

"Don't!" she enjoined. "Chuck it—you look such a silly fool!" She thrust him away, and rearranged her disordered hair. She was not by any means afraid of him; wasn't he only a poor, wretched half-caste? But at the same time she didn't want him; didn't like the odour of his oily black hair which was right under her nose, or the reek of stale smoke that hung about his dress-suit. She skipped out of his reach, and cocked a little finger at him, while she sang, light-heartedly:

"I love you, little yellow bird, But I love my libertee!"

Like a yellow wraith Cheng Brander faded into the night, his face and gait calm and inscrutable. Before him danced the face of Jewell Angell, like a lamp lit by the pure candour of her character: Jewell Angell, the lady partner in the music hall acrobatic turn of Diabolo and Angela.

He walked home, suffering an overmastering desire to hurt this beautiful, frail thing that had called him Yellow Rat. To strike her physically would, he knew, be useless; these fool English did not understand that women might justifiably be struck; and also, Jewell was, by her profession, too hard and sturdy, for all her appearance of frailty, to be hurt by any blow that he could deliver on her body. But there were, perchance, other ways. His half-Oriental brain uncoiled itself from its sensuous sloth and glided through a strange forest of ideas, and Cheng Brander slept that night in the bosom of this forest.

Next evening, as musical director of the dusty, outmoded theatre of varieties, he climbed to his chair, his blinking face as impassive as ever, his hand as steady. Some of the boys in the orchestra had often objected to working under a yellow peril, but he was a skilled musician, and the management kept him on because he drew to the hall the Oriental element of the quarter. He ducked from below, slid to his chair, and, on the tinkle of the stage manager's bell, took up his baton, tapped, and led the boys through some rag-tag overture.

Diabolo and Angela were fourth call, and at the moment of the overture they were in their dressing-rooms, making up. Their turn consisted of an eccentric gymnastic display, culminating in a sensational drop by Diabolo from a trapeze fixed in the flies to a floating trapeze on the stage. The drop involved two somersaults, and the space and the moment must be nicely calculated so that his hands should arrive in precise juxtaposition with the swing of the lower trapeze. Every movement in the turn and the placing of every piece of property was worked out to the quarter-inch. The heightening or lowering of either trapeze, by the merest shade, would make a difference in the extent of his reach and might turn the double fall into disaster. Everything being fixed in the usual way—and he always personally superintended the fixing of his props—Diabolo knew exactly when to fall and how far to swing out. He would wait for *The Bridal Chorus*, catch the tact of the music in his pulses, and the rest was automatic, or, at any rate, subconscious. On the first note of a certain bar, he would swing off and arrive a second later, on the lower bar. For five years he had done the trick thus, and never once had he erred. It was as easy as stepping off the pavement; and so perfectly drilled were his muscles and nerve centres that he got no thrill of any kind out of his evening's work.

The call-boy shot a bullet head through Diabolo's door, and cried for band parts. They were flung at him—band parts composed of a medley of popular airs. He returned ten minutes later.

"The Six Italias are on, sir."

"Right-o!" said Diabolo, and descended the stone stairs. In the wings he met Jewell, and they moved round the front cloth, before which a girl was snarling and dancing and divulging the fact that her wardrobe was of the scantiest. They moved among their props, pulling at this, altering that, and swearing at the stage hands, who accepted curses as other men accept remarks about the weather.

"Hope that yellow pussy'll get your changes a bit smarter tonight," said Jewell. "Did I tell you the little perisher's been after me? Yep. . . . Fancy thinking I'd take him on! Fresh little greaser! Mauled me about, too. I pretty quick dropped it across him, you bet."

"Good," said Johnnie. "I'll pull his yeller face to bits if he comes round you while I'm about. Tell him from me he'd best stop trifling with suicide. Better ring through, p'r'aps, and tell him to follow our marks on the score. Here—Fred—ring the band, will you, and tell him Diabolo and Angela want him to watch out for their cues, 'cos he mucked 'em last night. Tell him we change to Number Five directly I'm up the rope."

They drew back to the wings as the seriocomic girl kicked a clumsy and valedictory leg over the footlights and fell against the entrance curtain. They heard their symphony being blared by the brass, and then, with that selfsufficient, mincing gait traditional to the acrobat, they tripped on.

It was a poor house—a Tuesday night house—thin and cold. They did not go well; and while Diabolo was doing the greater share of the stunts, Jewell stood against the back-cloth, with arms behind her in the part of the attendant sprite. From there she was looking into the bleak, blank face of Cheng Brander, and she thought that a baboon might wag a baton with as much intelligence. His attitude in the chair was always the same: negligent, scornful. He saw nothing from his Olympian detachment, looked at none of the turns, smiled at none of their quips, but leant back in his chair at a comfortable angle, his elbow resting on the arm, his wrist directing the beat of the baton, his glance fixed either on the score or wandering to the roof.

Following a brilliant display of jugglery with Indian clubs, Johnnie bowed and danced himself upstage, whence, by a pulley-rope, he was hauled to the flies. Jewell mouthed at the stage manager in the wings. The stage manager spoke through the telephone, and Cheng Brander, bending to the receiver, listened:

"Number Five," said the voice to Cheng Brander.

"Number Nine," said Cheng Brander to his men.

"One! Two! Three!" cried the voice of Johnnie from the flies. The audience could just perceive his head, as he swung by the legs from the upper trapeze.

"Number Nine," Cheng Brander had said, and the band blared, not *The Bridal Chorus*, but *Stars and Stripes*. Johnnie was swinging in rhythm to a melody with which he was so familiar that he was expecting it before a bar was to be heard. He was anticipating the beat of *The Bridal Chorus*, and the muscles of his legs had, of their own accord, slacked their hold on the bar in readiness for the exact moment of release, when his ears told him of a mistake. Something was wrong somewhere—something—something. . . . In a fraction of a second he realised that the beat of the music was not the beat to which his nerves were keyed. In a fraction of a second he tried to recover, to check the incipient fall. But his nerves, thrown out of gear by this unexpected rhythm at such a moment, failed to respond. The trapeze swung forward. His hands clutched air. His legs went limp. He came down on his head. One heard a muffled blow as of something cracking.

A short, sharp gasp came from the house. Cheng bent forward and peered across the lights. The curtain fell, and the house rose, sick and disquieted. As it fell, the woman rushed downstage, and bent with fond hands and inarticulate cries over the body of her boy.

"The man's dead," said Cheng. "The show's stopped. Play them out with *The Chinese Patrol*." He raised his baton, and his face was grave and inscrutable, save for a tiny flickering at the yellow eyelids, which told that he was very, very happy.

BERYL, THE CROUCHER
AND THE REST OF ENGLAND

IT is an episode in the life and death of Beryl Hermione Maud Chudder and of Croucher Stumpley, and it is told because it is beautiful, and because the rest of England arose in its fat, satin'd, Bayswater wrath, and called it beastly. Horrid things have to be told with it, as with all tales of Limehouse; but hear the story, if you will, and be gentle, be pitiful.

The Croucher, known also as the Prize Packet and the Panther, was only a boy, just nineteen; and when he quitted the ring one Saturday night at Netherlands, after a heavy and fast fifteen rounds, in which only the gong had saved his opponent from the knockout, it was with a free mind, careless of the future, joyful in the present. He had no fight in view for another two months; therefore he could cut loose a bit, for, in wine or want, he was always gay. There had, then, been drinks after the fight—several; but it was the last that did the trick—an overripe gin. It had made him ill, and he had slouched away from the boys to be ill quietly. Now he wanted something to pull him together again, for he thought—as one does think after three or four—that five or six might do the trick; so behold him, at ten-thirty on this Saturday night, loafing along East India Dock Road, and turning into Pennyfields. From Pennyfields he drifted over West India Dock Road, passed a house where a window seemed deliberately to wink at him, and so swung into that Causeway where the cold fatalism of the Orient meets the wistful dubiety of the West. Here he was known and popular with the Chinkies, for he was a quiet lad, with nothing of bombast, and liked to talk with them. Besides, he was famous. He had knocked out Nobby Keeks, the Limehouse Wonder, and had once had Seaman Hunks in serious difficulties for ten rounds, though matched above his weight; and altogether was regarded as a likely investment by the gang that backed him.

In the Causeway all was secrecy and half tones. The winter's day had died in a wrath of flame and cloud, and now pinpoints of light pricked the curtain of mist. The shuttered gloom of the quarter showed strangely menacing. Every whispering house seemed an abode of dread things. Every window seemed filled with frightful eyes. Every corner, half lit by the bleak light of a naked gas-jet, seemed to harbour unholy things, and a sense of danger hung on every step. The Causeway was just a fog of yellow faces and labial murmurings.

The Croucher entered the little bar at the corner. The company was poor: two bashful Chinkies and two dock drunks. As he strode in, one of the drunks was talking in tones five sizes larger than life. The landlord was maintaining his reputation for *suaviter in modo* by informing him at intervals that he was a perfect bloody nuisance to any respectable house, and the sooner he drank up and cleared and never came near his bar again, the better; while his pal attended to the *fortiter in re* by prodding him repeatedly over the kidneys.

"Well, if yer want a woman, have a woman, and shut up about it."

"Aw right. I'll give ten bob for one tonight—there!" And with a proud hand he jumped a half-sovereign on the table and caught it.

The Croucher had a brandy, and followed the conversation without listening. He was, as he said, off-colour. Bad-tempered about everything, like, and didn't know why. Everything was all *right*. But . . . well, he just felt like that. He wanted something to happen. Something new. His thoughts swam away like roving fish, and came back suddenly, as the roaring of the two drunks dropped. It was one of the Chinks who was talking now, in a whisper:

"Ah said get you one for twelve shillings."

The drunk thrust up a distorted jaw and stared at him. The stare was meant to be strong and piercing; it was merely idiotic.

"What's she like?"

"Dark. Heap plitty."

"Give you ten bob."

"No. Twelve shillings. Nice gel."

"Where's she come from? How long you had her?"

Now the Croucher pricked up his ears and butted in. He had an idea. Here was something that might amuse him for a bit, and take off that sickish feeling. A nice girl. . . . Good fun. Yes, rather. He had wanted something fresh, some kind of excitement to stir things up a bit. He felt better already.

"'Ere, Chinky," he called. "Leave that blasted drunk and come over here. Got somethink for yeh."

The blasted drunk got up, by a grip on the Chink's coat tail, and mentioned that he'd show kids whether they could insult a perfly respectable sailor by . . . He then saw that the kid was the Croucher, and his mate pulled him back, and he slid off the seat and was no more heard of.

"Look here, Chinky," murmured Croucher, "I'll . . . what you going to have? Right-o. Two brandies, quick. . . . Is this all right, this gel?"

"Sh! Les. Always all light with Wing Too, eh?"

"Well, listen. I'm on to that. See?"

Wing Foo slid aside, and conferred with his fat yellow friend.

"All light," he agreed, returning to the Croucher. "You come 'long now, and see her. You have my room, les."

The three slid into the Causeway together. The air was busy with the wailing of a Chinese fiddle. All about them was gloom; twilit shops; snatches of honeyed talk; fusty smells; bits of traffic; seamen singing. They crossed the road, slipped Pennyfields, and came to the house set with its back to the corner whose single window had winked at the Croucher a few minutes past.

The door yielded at a push, and they entered the main room, lit by a forlorn candle. The elder Chink extended a fiat hand. The Croucher filled it with thirty pieces of silver, and the bargain was made. One of them disappeared, and a moment or so later the purchase appeared at the foot of the stairs which led from the fireplace. On seeing the Croucher her colour grew, and she gave a quick gasp of surprise which was unnoticed by the Chinks. But the Croucher caught it. Beryl Hermione Maud was dark and just fourteen; a neat little figure, not very tall for her age, but strangely intuitive, overripe, one might say. Morally, she had grown too fast. Though only fourteen years were marked in the swift lines of her form, in her face were all the wisdom and all the tears of the ages. She was one of those precocities which abound in this region. She had a genius for life, for divining its mysteries, where others wait on long years of experience. Her father had said that she was a fast little bitch because she stayed out late and lengthened her skirts, and he threatened to wallop her if she didn't behave herself. She then made the mistake of assuming that this new dignity afforded her the protection of maturity, and proceeded to further liberties. Her father made haste to shake her belief in this idea, and to remind her that she was only fourteen, by turning up those lengthened skirts and giving her the spanking she deserved. This so exasperated her that she ran away from Tidal Basin, and here she was with the yellow men.

She really was a dainty production. Not beautiful in the Greek sense, for there is nothing more tedious than the Greek idea of beauty and proportion. Beryl Hermione Maud's beauty was more interesting; indefinite, wayward. The features were irregular, but there was some quality in the face that called you back. To look into it was to look into the solemn deeps of a cathedral. Only the lips held any touch of grossness. Her skin was translucent and fine. Her thick loaded curls tumbled to her neck. Her glances were steady and reticent, and in her movements was the shy dignity of the child.

The Croucher was fairly drunk by this time, but he was sober enough to look at her and discover that she was desirable, and had great joy to give to men. He swayed across to her, and put his steely arms about her white neck. She greeted him with a smile, and remained limp and passive under his embrace, her face lifted, expectant. A shudder ran about her of delight, fear, and wonder. He was about to seal the bargain with an unholy kiss when through the hush of the hour came the crack of a revolver shot.

All started. A moment later came a great shout, and then a babble. There was chorus of many feet. The noise swelled to a broad roar, the feet came faster.

Smack! came a stone at the window, and a trickling of broken glass. The Croucher swung away from Beryl Hermione Maud and looked out. A man, his whole body insane with fear, was running to the house; behind him was a nightmare of pursuers. Five seconds, and he was at the door. Without knowing why, the Croucher pulled it open. The man collapsed in the little room. The Croucher shut the door.

"Good Gawd, the ol' man!"

"Let yer old dad in, boy! Gimme a chance! . . . Oh, Gawd. They nearly 'ad me. I done a murder. Just 'ad time to run. Old Borden told me you'd gone with the Chinks. 'Elp me, boy, 'elp me. Don't let 'em git me. They'll 'ang me. 'Ang me. Oh, Christ—they're *coming!*" His voice rose to a scream. "Don't go back on me. Gimme a chance to hide. Keep 'em back while I get wind. I can't run no more. Go out, and 'it 'em, boy. You can. Stand by yer dad!"

But the Croucher was not wanting these appeals. Already he had dragged the old man up, and sat him in a chair. Now there was a fury of police whistles spurting into the night like water on a fire. The anger of the streets came to them in throbbing blasts. The Croucher slipped to the window. From under his coat he drew a Smith-Wesson. The old man stretched a stupid hand.

"D-d-d-don't! Don't shoot 'em. Fight 'em!"

"Blast you—and shut up!" snapped the Croucher. "It's all right. It'll just stop 'em. It's blanks."

He raised the gun to the broken pane and fired, twice. It did stop 'em. It wasn't blank. It was ball.

The leading officer went down and out. The next man took his bullet in the thigh. Both tumbled ridiculously, and the crowd behind gyrated on them like a bioscope "comic." Those who were able sorted themselves out and ran zealously home. The others remained to struggle and to pray.

"Bloody fool!" cried the old man. "You done it now. Oh, Christ. We both done a murder now. Gawd 'elp us!"

"Damn good job!"

Stumpley, the elder, collapsed in his chair again, his face white and damp with sweat. The Chinks waited, as ever, impassive. The Croucher stood out, alert, commanding.

"Bolt the door," said the Croucher.

"Clamp the windows," said the Croucher.

"Light the lamp," said the Croucher.

The door was bolted, the windows clamped, the lamp lit. The four men regarded one another. Behind them, in the shaking shadow, stood Beryl Hermione Maud. Then the Croucher saw her. "Send the girl upstairs," he said; and she went.

It was a curious situation. The Chinks didn't give a damn either way. They were all in for a picnic now—or something worse than a picnic—if there is anything worse. Life or death—it was all one to them. The old man had killed someone; he would be hanged. The boy had killed someone; he would be hanged. They would be charged with harbouring, and facts about the little girl, and about other business of theirs would come out. So, as there would be trouble any way, they were quite prepared to take what came. Then there was the old man, palsied with fright, hoping, antici-pating, hysterical and inarticulate. Then there was the Croucher, in love with life, but game enough to play his part and keep his funk locked tightly inside him. Finally there was the girl, who—but what she felt is but a matter for conjecture. So far, she had shown about as much emotion as any girl of her age shows when the music-teacher arrives. The others took a clear atti-tude on the situation. She was a dark horse. Indeed, she might just as well not have been there, and, so far as the men were concerned, she was not. She was simply forgotten.

They sent her upstairs and left her, while they argued and fought and barricaded. But she must have thought hard and lived many hard years during those two days of the Swatow Street siege, when she waited in the upper room, forlorn and helpless.

Presently one of the Chinks retired and came back with two revolvers and a small tin box.

"Guns," he said simply.

"Gimme a shot o' dope," slobbered the old man. "Gimme a jolt, Chinky."

The Croucher stared at the guns. "Oh. Going to 'ave a run for yer money, old cock? Well, we're all in, now. Only a matter o' time. They're bound to win in the end. Tip out the bunce, old sport. Ball, all the time. If they're going to take me alive, they'll lose half-a-dozen of their boys first. They're all round the back now. I 'eard 'em. We can't get out. It's rope for me and dad. And it's a stretch for you two. Round to the back, you Chinky. Keep the window and the door. Good job I'm drunk. You—up to the back window. Watch for ladders. We'll show 'em something."

He did. You will recall the affair. How the police surrounded that little Fort Chabrol. How the deadly aim of the half-drunk Croucher and the cold Chinkies got home on the Metropolitan Police Force again and again. How the Croucher worked the front of the house, which faces the whole length of the street, and how the Chinkies took the back and the roof. How the police, in their helplessness against such fatalistic defiance of their authority, appealed to Government, and how the Government sent down a detachment of the Guards. You will recall how, in the great contest of four men and a girl v. the Rest of England, it was the Rest of England that went down. The overwhelming minority quietly laughed at them. Of course, you cannot kill an English institution with ridicule, for ridicule presupposes a sense of proportion in the thing ridiculed; but there was another way by which the lonely five put the rest of England to confusion.

It was all very wicked. Murder had been done. It is impossible to justify the situation in any way. In Bayswater and all other haunts of unbridled chastity the men and the girl were tortured, burnt alive, stewed in oil, and submitted to every conceivable pain and penalty for their saucy effrontery. Yet somehow, there was a touch about the whole thing, this spectacle of four men defying the whole law and order of the greatest country in the world, that thrilled every man with any devil in him.

It thrilled the Croucher. The theatricality of it appealed irresistibly to him. Just then, he lived gloriously. While old Stumpley snivelled and convulsed, he and his Chinks put up a splendid fight. Through a little air-hole of the shuttered window Croucher wrought his will on all invaders, and when the Guards erected their barricade at the end of the street he roared.

Zpt! Zpt! Zpt! Their rifles spat vicious death, and tinkles of glass and plaster announced the coming of the bullets. But, by the irony of things, the defenders remained untouched.

*   *   *

It was on the night of the second day that the Croucher began to be tired, and to feel that things must be ended. He and the Chinks had accepted the situation, and had kicked old man Stumpley into a corner.

Then they had taken turns in watching and sleeping. The rest of England had kept up a desultory *plopetty-plop-plop* at their blockhouse, bringing down bits of plaster and woodwork and other defenceless things. But it could not go on for ever; and two days of siege, with constant gripping of a gun, is too much for the nerves, even when you know that death is at the end of it. He did not fancy walking out and being shot down, though this is what the old man wished to do; in fact they had had to hold him down in his chair that very morning to prevent him. He did not fancy the inglorious death of a self-directed bullet; and he certainly was not going to a mute surrender and the farce of an Old Bailey trial. He asked something larger, something with more . . .

He then discovered that his thoughts were running in the same track as on the night that began the trouble, and association of ideas at once brought the girl to his mind. Gawd! Here he was going out, and he hadn't had his time, his damfinold time that he had promised himself. After all, he might as well have his penn'orth. He'd done murder, which was the worst thing you could do. So he might just as well get some fun out of lesser offences. What-o! It happened to be his turn to watch; but he might just as well have company for the watch; and, anyway, there was nothing to watch for. There, before them, was the whole of English civilisation, holding back in fear of four men with a large supply of cartridges. England hoped to starve them into surrender so that it could hang them comfortably; that much of their tactics he had divined. So—on with the dance! And then—Ta-ta!

He slipped upstairs to the room where they had locked Beryl Hermione Maud, lest she might make trouble. He unlocked the door and entered.

It is not definitely known what happened at that interview. He was there some while, and, when he came down, he came down, not gay and light-hearted, as he had gone, but morose, changed. Something in his face, in his manner, had altered. It was as though he had tightened up. He moved about as a man pondering on something which he is near to solving. The subject of his pondering was Beryl Hermione Maud. For this had happened—in those few full moments he had awakened to the meaning of love.

When he awoke in the late morning, after relief by Wing Foo, he learned that his old dad was lying in the roadway just outside. He had dashed out before either could stop him, and had gone down to half-a-dozen shots.

That settled it. They might as well finish their cartridges and then finish the whole thing. They might as well——

What the hell was that coming downstairs? Smell it? Burning—eh? Smoke—look at it! Gawd!

The Croucher leapt upstairs.

He leapt upstairs to Beryl Hermione Maud. But the smoke came from her room. He roared at the door and dashed upon it. It swung open. Flame alone held it. She was gone. Then he turned, and saw her on the narrow landing, choking and blinking through a cloud of smoke, as in a dream.

"What the bloody——Come outer that!" he yelled, and grabbed her sleeve. "Quick—it'll be on us in a minute." He shoved her before him to the stairs, but she drew back. "Who done it?" he gasped.

"No—no. Stop. I done it. There was some paraffin in the cupboard there. And some matches. I started the wall where the paper was loose. It'll be through in a jiffy. . . . No, I ain't going down."

"What the devil . . . What the——Don' be a fool. You can get out. I'll come wiv yer. Quick—it's catching the stairs!"

There they stood in the golden haze, while tongues of flame lisped wickedly about them. The heat was insufferable, the smoke asphyxiating. Suddenly, through the crackling of wood, came a revolver shot. The Croucher leaned over the crazy banister. Wing Foo had found honourable death.

Beryl Hermione Maud softly touched his arm. "Come in here. This room. It'll get here last." Something in her voice, her gesture, struck him silly. He couldn't have commanded at that moment. He obeyed.

When in the little room, she shut the door, and snakes of smoke crawled under it. Then she stepped quietly to him, put her hands about his face, and kissed him.

* * *

There, virtually, the story ends, though much happened between them before their course was run. There was talk, curious talk, the talk of a woman of thirty to the man of her life, monstrous to hear from a child to a boy of nineteen. There were embraces, garrulous silences, kisses, fears and tremblings. In those moments the Croucher awoke to a sense of the bigness of things. He became enveloped in something . . . a kind of . . . well, the situation and—oh, everything. The murder, the siege, all London waiting for him, and that sort of thing. It gave him a new emotion; he felt proud and clean all through. He felt, in his own phrase, like as though he was going to find something he'd been hunting for for years and forgotten.

One would like to know more, perhaps, for it might help us to live, and teach us something of pity. But it is not to be known; and, after all, these were the little moments of their lives, sacred to themselves. One can conjecture what passed—the terribly inspired things that were said, the ridiculously tragic things that were done. One guesses that the Croucher stood mazed and dumb and blustering with gesture as Beryl stretched impassioned hands to him and screamed that she loved him, had loved him for years, as he went conqueringly about Limehouse, and that she had fired the house that they might die together.

And one knows what happened in the last three minutes, for the wide window fell, and those below saw clearly. The front of the house was a mouth of flame. The troops and police closed in. A fire engine jangled insanely at the end of Pekin Street. People shouted. People screamed. And they heard Beryl Hermione Maud speak.

"Open the door. It'll be over quicker. Kiss me, Croucher."

They saw the Croucher open the door and spring again to her side, as an octopus of fire writhed upon them. A police officer yelled obscure advice. A fireman dashed forward and grew suddenly frantic, for though everything was at hand, nothing could be done. The nearest hydrant was many yards away, and the engine had to make a circuit. Even the pressmen were momentarily awed.

Beryl flung furious arms about her boy, and again was heard to speak. "You afraid?"

"Wiv you? Christ Almighty, no. But . . . oh . . . you . . . young . . . wonderful . . . ought to live. 'Tain't fair. It's bloody. You ain't had your time . . . and you ain't done nothing wrong. I deserve what I got, but . . . Steady—it's coming now."

They saw him pull her back on his arm. They saw him put a large hand over her mouth and drag her where the smoke rolled.

*   *   *

"Easy—hoses!"

"Stir up, damyeh. Lively, there."

"Finished with engine."

"Stand clear, dammit, stand clear. Salvage up."

"Take report, Simpson. Smart now. Two bodies . . ."

"Oh, dammit, do stand clear!"

THE SIGN OF THE LAMP

HERE, O hearts that beat with mine, is the saddest of all tales. It is the tale of the breaking of a man's faith in woman. A thousand arrows over their places of slumber. . . .

It was on the Bund of Shanghai that the father of Sway Lim had said these words to him: "Son, mistrust all white women; they are but pale devils; they shall ensnare you."

But Lim had not listened; and it was Poppy Sturdish, of Limehouse and Poplar, who proved to him that his father spoke truth. Poppy was fair in the eyes of a Chinaman; she was an anaemic slip of a girl, with coarse skin and mean mouth, a frightened manner and a defiant glance. She had scarce any friends, for she was known to be a copper's nark; thus came the fear in her step and the challenge in her eyes. Often she had blown the gaff on the secret games of Chinatown, for she spoke Cantonese and a little Swahili and some Hindustani, and could rustle it with the best of them; and it was her skill and shrewdness in directing the law to useful enterprises, such as the raiding of wicked houses, that caused her to be known in all local stations and courts as the Chinese Poppy.

She lived in the tactfully narrow Poplar High Street, that curls its nasty length from Limehouse to Blackwall, and directly opposite her cottage was the loathly lodging of Sway Lim—one room, black and smelly with dirt—next the home of the sailors of Japan. From his open window he could see into the room of the desirable Poppy, and by day and evening he would sit there, watching her movements, and listening with delight to her chief charm—that voice of hers that wailed in your heart long since it had ceased to wail in your ears. She was a bad girl, mean and treacherous; everybody knew that; but she was young and very pale; so that Sway Lim, wet-lipped, would gloat upon her from his window. Sometimes he would pluck at his plaintive fiddle, and make a song for her. Over the sad, yellow evening his voice would float in an old Malayan chanty:

"Love is kind to the least of men. . . . *Eee-awa! Eee-awa!*"

But a little while, and she had consented to walk with Lim, and to visit the Queen's Theatre, and to take drinks—double gins—at the Blue Lantern. From him she accepted brooches and rings wherewith to deck the beauty of her twenty-five years; and when she questioned him whence he had the money for these things, he told her that he played fan-tan at the house of Ho Ling. This he did either not knowing or not caring that Poppy was a

55

copper's nark, and was under the sharp thumb of an inspector. He talked to Poppy as he had talked to none outside his native land. He told her of his home, of his childhood, of his prolific and wonderful parent, who had twelve mighty sons. He talked of a land of lilies and soft blue nights which he had left that he might adventure in strange countries, and see the beauties of the white girls of other lands, and learn great things, as befitted the first son of a proud house. He told her how well he played fan-tan, where he played it, and at what times, how many tricks he had acquired, and the heap plenty money he had made. And he sang to her: *Yao chien wo ngai tzu nu.*

All these things he told her in successive sweet evenings of June, when Limehouse was a city of rose and silver, and the odour of exotic spices lured every sense to the secret amiable delights of the pillow. All these things he told her; yet was he surprised when one night there came a knocking at the lower door of the house of Ho Ling, and a knocking at the back door of the house of Ho Ling, and a knocking at the upper door of the house of Ho Ling, and the ominously casual entrance of burly gentlemen in racing overcoats, bowler hats, and large boots. He was surprised when he was hauled away to a station, and detained for the night in the cells, and taken thence to Thames Police Court. Was he surprised when he saw the Chinese Poppy in court, chatting affably with the most important-looking gentleman in racing overcoat and bowler hat? He was not. His heart broke within him, and all emotion died. Tears came to his throat, but not to his eyes, so that when the interpreter questioned him, he could make no answer; his dignity dropped from him; he could but glare and mumble. "I loved her," his heart cried silently; "I loved her, and she betrayed me. Treachery. Treachery." And his companions in the dock, who, too, had warned him against the white girl, wagged wise, condemnatory heads that would have declared: "We told you so."

His heart was broken by a white barbarian devil of a girl; and he addressed himself forthwith, quietly and tenderly, to vengeance. He paid his fine, and those of his companions, for he alone had sufficient money to save them from prison; and then he went home to his chamber, walking to a monotonous march of: "Treachery. Treachery." As he turned into Poplar High Street he came upon Poppy, walking with a beefy youth, who glowered and looked very strong. As Poppy passed, she lifted a slim, white hand, smacked the face of Sway Lim and, with delicate, cruel fingers, pulled the nose of Sway Lim.

It was enough. If a broken heart had not been enough, then this assault had crowned it. His holy of holies, his personal dignity, his nose, had been degraded. All the wrath of his fathers foamed in his blood. All the tears of the ages rushed over his heart. Innumerable little agonies scorched his flesh. Silently, swiftly, he crouched into himself as a tortoise into its shell, and, followed by the brute laughter of the beefy youth, he slipped by dark corners away.

Once in his chamber, he bowed himself before the joss, and burned many prayer papers that the powers might be propitiated and pleased to forward his schemes.

*   *   *

Now it was not long before the gentle, wet lips of Sway Lim had won from other lips, less gentle, but well moistened with beer and gin, certain things good to be known concerning Poppy Sturdish, or Chinese Poppy. He learnt that her heart and the beautiful body of her, loaded with infinite pale graces that never a yellow man might discover, had been freely rendered to another; not to the Inspector, but to a greater personage of Poplar: none other than the beefy youth, Hunk Bottles.

Hunk Bottles was not a good man. The life he led was not clean. He robbed and bashed. It was rumoured that he had done worse deeds, too, by night; but, as the leader of the Hunk Bottles Gang, and the sower of strife among the labourers, white, black, brown and yellow, of the docks, he was a fellow of some consequence, and there were times when the police looked steadily in the opposite direction when he approached.

But there was at last a day when public sentiment demanded that all local and personal considerations be set aside, and that Hunk Bottles be apprehended. For it had come to pass that murder had been done in Chinatown, in a nasty house near Pennyfields, where men played cards and other games, and sometimes quarrelled among themselves; and the police sought the murderer and found him not. Only they found in the hand of the murdered man half the sleeve of a coat: a coat of good material, a material which a local tailor recognised because he used very little of it, and had but two customers for it. One was his own father; the other was Hunk Bottles.

But Hunk Bottles had flown, and none knew whither. Yet were there two who could have made very shrewd guesses. One of these sat, with a broken heart, evening by evening, at his window, watching the opposite window, where sometimes a soft shape would dance across the blind, and dance with trampling feet upon his poor heart. Sometimes the door would open, and she would go forth, and he would watch her, and when she was gone, he would continue to watch the way she was gone, and would sit until she returned. Sometimes her window would open, too, and she would shoot a spiteful head through it, and cry to him, in her own rich tongue, that all yellow swine were offal to her. This man knew where Hunk Bottles might be found, for he had seen Hunk Bottles creep to the opposite door, at the dark hour of two in the morning, and he had seen a lowered light, had heard the crackle of a whisper, and the sweet hiss of stormy kisses showered upon the white body of Poppy, and her murmurous defiance: "I won't give you up. Never. Never. Never. Take me dyin' oath I won't. Not if they kill me, Hunk. 'Ope I'm in 'ell first."

Very swiftly the story spread through Limehouse from gentle Chinese lips, and it came, in less than an hour, to the police station. Fifteen minutes later the important gentleman in racing overcoat and bowler hat called upon Poppy, and challenged her. And when he had challenged her, he charged her with a mission. At first she was truculent; then sullen; then complacent. She took her dyin' oath that she didn't know where Hunk was. She only knew that he had been to her twice, very late at night. She did not know where he came from, or where he went. She was in deadly fear of him. Of course she ought to have give him up, but how could she? He'd split her throat. He carried a gun and knives. He'd do her in at once if he suspected. What *could* she do?

They talked . . . and talked. The Inspector's large hand moved emphatically, patting the table as he made certain points.

"Don't try to tell me," he urged, in the off-hand way of the police officer. "I know all about it. You do what you got to do, and you needn't be frightened of nobody. And you better do it, I give you my word, me gel; I got you fixed good and tight. So watch out. And don't forget nothing. Now then . . . what's your orders?"

In a dull, cold voice Poppy repeated a formula. "Put the lamp in the window, with the red shade on. When I got his gun and his two knives off him, I take the shade away. Then you comes in."

"That's it. Why, it's as easy. . . . Just a little lovey-lovey. Kinder lead him on. Then sit him down on that there sofa, and love him some more. Then he'll take off his belt, and other things. When he's got his coat off, with the gun in it, get him over this side away from it. Never mind about the knives; he won't get a chanst to use them. Then you put your hand up, to straighten your hair, like, and knock the shade off, accidental.

"Now mind yeh. . . . No hanky-panky. Else I'll have to do it on yeh, as

I ought to have done years ago. So mind yeh. I ain't standing any khybosh. Not in these nor any other trousers. You do what you're told, and things'll be all the better for you for a long time to come. We shall be outside from now till he comes. So don't try to slip out and bung him the word. It won't be no good. And above all, don't try to get gay with me. See? Ever read your Bible? Read it now, 'fore he comes. There's a yarn about a chap called Samson, and his gel Delilah. Tells you just how to do it!"

He had just snapped his last phrase when there came to both of them, very sharp and clear, the wailing of a Malayan chanty:

"Love is kind to the least of men. . . . *Eee-awa! Eee-awa!*"

Instinctively both looked up, and then they saw that the window was wide to the street, and at the opposite open window was a yellow face and head which blinked at them impassively under the hard morning light, and continued its melancholy entertainment. A few long hours followed, and then came Hunk Bottles, perilously, slipperily. He was whisked into the house as by a gust of wind, while in several grim corners several gentlemen in racing overcoats and bowler hats, and one in uniform, grinned quietly. For now it was Poppy's charge to deliver the boy to his tormentors, and she should very terribly cop out if she failed in that charge.

That, however, was exactly what she meant to do. He had come, her own, very own Hunk; and she must get him away. Hunk and herself would escape or die together; and, if they died, several gentlemen in racing overcoats and bowler hats should die with them. There was a back entrance to her little house. The Inspector had not thought to post men there; after all, she was a copper's nark, and he assumed that he had fairly frightened her by his instructions that morning. He had overlooked the fact that Poppy was a London girl, and that she loved Hunk Bottles. He had forgotten that the state of love is so very near to the state of death.

The moment Hunk was in her room, she spoke swift words to him. She told him of his peril; she told him of the instructions given to her. She repeated her oath of allegiance, and detailed her plan for escape.

"They'll have to kill me first, Hunk. Sop me gob they will. I'm never going back on yeh. Never!" And she flung hot little arms about him, letting him play with her as he would while he urged her to pull herself together. When she had finished assaulting his scrubby face with wet kisses, she asked him if he had got his gun and his two knives, and he assured her that he had, as well as a knuckle-duster. And she asked him if he would make a fight for it if they were caught, and he said he would, and groaned aloud when she forced him to promise that, if the fight were lost, he would put her out before the cops could get her. They embraced again, and he sobbed soft things to her beauty and her faithfulness.

Then she took the lamp from the table, set the red shade very firmly upon it, and placed it in the window.

"Half-a-mo', Hunk," she whispered. "I'll just slip away to the back, and make sure all's clear." She turned her face up to him as she retreated, and its pallor shone as though some sudden lamp of life had been lit within her, and a lonely Chinky at the opposite window groaned in his heart that no woman had ever given such a look to him.

But his face remained impassive, and, the moment she was gone from the room, he thrust across the narrow street a stiff, straight wire such as is used for fishing on the Great Yellow River, and so finely drawn that nothing could be seen of it in the road below.

Of a sudden the red shade of the lamp was twitched off.

Swiftly from their corners came several gentlemen in racing overcoats and bowler hats, one of whom carried a key. The door of the house was opened, and they disappeared. Ten seconds later they stood before Hunk Bottles, and Sway Lim at his window, breathing the scents of manioc and pickled eggs, saw them very clearly. He saw the sudden dismay on the face of the prisoner, and heard the sharp cry: "Copped, be Christ!" And then: "So she went to fetch yeh, the bitch!"

He saw him drop both hands in a gesture of surrender, and step forward. At the same moment, in the doorway appeared the pale, anguished figure of Poppy. She grasped the situation, and a spasm in her face showed that she grasped the awful construction that Hunk had placed upon it. She raised a protesting hand. Her lips moved as if to speak.

But Hunk, his face on fire with fury, grief and despair at this assumed betrayal by the woman he loved, waved her coldly away. He took his gun from his pocket, and handed it to the Inspector, who had held him covered. Poppy darted forward, but was dragged back. She screamed. Then, mercifully, she fainted; and did not hear, across the cruel night, a ripple of cold Oriental laughter and a voice that wailed an old Malayan chanty:

"Love is kind to the least of men. . . . *Eee-awa! Eee-awa!*"

TAI FU AND PANSY GREERS

NOW it came to pass that Mohammed Ali stood upon the steps of the Asiatics' Home and swore—not as you and I swear, but richly, with a feeling for colour and sting, strong in the vivid adjective. He swore in a bastard dialect compounded of Urdu, Chinese and Cocknese, and a swear skilfully dished up from these ingredients is—well, have you ever put cayenne on your mustard? Mohammed Ali was very cross, for his girl, his white girl, Pansy Greers, had given him the chuck, and for the reason which has brought many a good fellow the chuck—namely, lack of money.

Pansy was in trouble, and wanted money, of which he had none, for he was a destitute Oriental. Often they had gone about together, and in his way he had loved her. The girls of this quarter have a penchant for coloured boys, based, perhaps, on the attraction of repulsion. However, now that Mohammed Ali had failed her when put to the test, he was told that he need not again ask her to walk through Poplar Gardens. So he stood on the steps, and swore, while Pansy—

Well, Pansy was in trouble, and this was the way of it.

Pansy lived in Pekin Street. About her window the wires wove a network, and the beat of waters, as they slapped about the wharves, was day and night in her ears. At evenings there came to her the wail of the Pennyfields Orient, or the hysterical chortlings of an organ with music-hall ditties. She worked at Bennett's Cocoa Rooms in East India Dock Road; and life for her, as for most of her class, was just a dark house in a dark street. From the morning's flush to the subtle evening, she stood at steaming urns, breathing an air limp with the smell of food, and serving unhealthy eatables to cabmen, draymen, and, occasionally, a yellow or black or brown sailor.

She was not pretty. The curse of labour was on her face, and she carried no delicacies wherewith to veil her maidenhood. From dawn to dusk, from spring to spring, she had trodden the golden hours in this routine, and knew, yet scarcely felt, the slow sucking of her ripening powers. Twenty-one she was; yet life had never sung to her. Toil, and again toil, was all she knew—toil on a weakened body, improperly fed; for your work-girl of the East seldom knows how to nourish herself. Pansy lived, for the most part, on tea and sweets.

She was a good girl. Others of her set found escape and joys in many crude festivities—music halls, "hops," and brute embraces and kisses and intimacy with the boys. But she cared for none of these. Her friends allowed that she had no go, and hinted, with harsh indecencies, that if the truth were told your quiet ones were often worst. Her Sundays she spent tucked in bed with *East Lynne* or *Forget-Me-Not*; but, although her little head gloated on gilded sin, she had never once tasted it, for she loved but one human thing—her blowsy mother. Her mother, too, loved but one thing—not a human thing, but a bottled article—gin.

So, too soon, her mother came to die.

Pansy came home from the shop one night; climbed the stark stairs to their room; stopped to chi-ike the half-naked children playing on the landing. Murmuring a ragtime melody, she slouched in, and . . .

The room was dark, and she felt a sudden nameless chill.

She lit the lamp. Mother was dead.

Those that live, as Pansy did, all their days in physical contact with the brutality of things become too broken for complaint or remonstrance. This shock left Pansy just cold and numb, acceptant. It never occurred to her that hers was a hard lot, that life was not what it ought to be; vaguely she had stumbled on the truth of going on, whatever happened. So she went on. One thing alone spun dully on her brain, apart from the grief of losing her one pal, and that was—how to provide a funeral such as mother had always desired. For mother, after many years of gin, was sentimental. She wanted to be buried outside the parish, with her man. She wanted a brave show. A real handsome funeral, don't forget. Feathers, flowers, pall, and a nice sit-down for the guests afterwards. When, however, you have paid the rent, bought food and dressed yourself, there isn't much to save for burial out of eight-and-sixpence a week. Neighbours, who are always friends in Poplar, brought their little gifts of love; what they had, they gave; but that was still a long way from a really swell planting.

It was at this point that Pansy prayed. It is seldom that they pray about the docks: the bread-and-butter race is a hard one, and the pace is cruel, and any slackening means disqualification, and praying, as Pansy had said, real good praying, takes time and thought. But her praying was made, and sharp and clear there came to her an answer. She went to Mohammed Ali, and Mohammed Ali, as recorded, failed her. But . . . she remembered Tai Fu. She remembered a creeping, scrofulous thing that had once or twice come to the Cocoa Rooms, and leered damply upon her. Now, like so many of the settlers in the Chinese quarter, Tai Fu had money—lots of it. How they make their money in London is a mystery, but make it they do, probably at the fan-tan table when their flush compatriots come off the boats; and Tai Fu was reputed to be one of the richest, though he lived sparsely. Perhaps he was saving so as to realise a cherished dream of returning to his native river town, and spending his later days in tranquillity and some magnificence. Certainly he spent little, and his pen-yen was his one expense.

He was a dreadful doper. Sometimes he would chew betel nut or bhang or hashish, but mostly it was a big jolt of yen-shi, for he got more value from that. He was a connoisseur, and used his selected yen-shi and yen-hok as an Englishman uses a Cabanas.

The first slow inhalations brought him nothing, but, as he continued, there would come a sweet, purring warmth about the limbs. This effect was purely physical: the brain was left cold and awake, the thought uncoloured. But slowly, as the draws grew deeper, the details of the room would fade, there would be a soft thunder in the ears, his eyes would close, and about the head gathered a cloud of lilac, at first opaque, but gradually lightening in consistency till it became but a shy gauze. Then, with all control of the faculties in suspension, out of the nebula would swim infinite delicacies of phantasy and rhythm, of the ethereal reality of a rose-leaf. There would be faces, half revealed and half secret, under torrents of loaded curls; faces, now dusky, now strangely white; faces pure and haunting, and faces of creeping sin, floating without movement, fading and appearing. Faces sad almost to tears; then laughing, languishing faces; then cold, profound, animal faces—the faces of women, for the most part, but now and then faces of children and indeterminate faces.

As the stupor developed, it would bring music to the ears, and a sense of the glory of the immediate moment, when every tissue of the body would be keyed to a pitch of ecstasy almost too sweet to be borne. Then, with a squall of brass in the ears, the colour would change, and this time it would hold stranger allurements. The whole dream, indeed, built itself as one builds a sumptuous banquet of the blending of many flavours and essences, each course a subtle, unmarked progression on its predecessor.

The last stage of the dope-dream would be a chaos of music and a frenzy of frock and limb and curl against delirious backgrounds. Always the background was the Causeway, Orientalised. The little café would leap and bulge to a white temple, the chimney against the sky would sprout into a pagoda, and there would be the low pulsing of tom-toms. The street would sway itself out of all proportion, and grotesque staircases would dip to it from the dim-starred night; and it would be filled with pale girls, half-garbed in white and silver, and gold and blue.

Tai Fu had never known a white girl. He was a loathly creature, old and fat and steamy, and none of the girls would have him, for all his wealth. His attitude to the world was the cold, pitiless attitude of the overfed and the overwined. But it was of him that Pansy thought in her trouble, and when he called at the cocoa shop, she, sick-limbed and eyes a-blear, but still working, since there was nothing else she could do, and it killed thought—she told him her tale. He grinned, loose-lipped, with anticipation of delight. What she asked him, in effect, was: would he lend her the money for the funeral? And Tai Fu said at once that he would, if, that is, she . . .

Well, she was a good girl, but she loved her mother as she loved nothing else, human or celestial. A dying wish was to her more sacred than a social form.

She would. She did. Tai Fu got the white girl he had only known in hop-smoke.

She went to him that night at his house in the Causeway. He opened the door himself, and flung a low-lidded, wine-whipped glance about her that seemed to undress her where she stood, noting her fault and charm as one notes an animal. He did not love her; there was no sentiment in this business. Brute cunning and greed were in his brow, and lust was in his lips. He wanted her, and he had got her—quite cheaply, too.

She went to him; and she came away with some gold pieces. But in her face was a look of horror which she carries today.

What he did to her in the blackness of that curtained room of his had best not be imagined. But she came away with a deep, cold desire and determination to kill him—and she was not the kind of girl who lightly stains her finger with a crime of that colour. She came away with bruised limbs and body, with torn hair, and a face paled to death.

However, her vow was kept. Mother had her funeral, which drew crowds from everywhere. There were pickles and ham, and coffee and beer and tea, and plum cake and jam, and flowers and—oh, everything classy.

The morning following the impressive interment she cleared up the litter in her room, and went to work at the Cocoa Rooms.

"Sorry," said the proprietor, "but you can't come here no more. Sorry. But there's a lot of talk going about. One of the Chinks got drunk last night, and has been saying things; and lots of people seen you go to his house the other night. Sorry; but I kept you here, it'd smash me with the outdoor trade, straight. Sorry. Here—you better have your week's money. You'll easy get something else, I dessay. Sorry, but it's more'n I dare. Understand, doncher?"

Well, she did not get another job. All about Poplar, Limehouse and St. George's the wretched story had galloped, for Tai Fu had told what he had done to her, and it was a tale worth telling. She was a bad girl—she was abominable—that was clear. If she'd only gone wrong ordinary, it wouldn't have been so bad, but this . . .

Cruel starings whipped her eyes wherever she went. Many came, curiously, with sympathy, eager to know, and from every side she heard, hot-eared, the low refrain: "Ah, there's your quiet ones! Now, didn't I only say—eh?—don't that just show?"

She did not get another job. Here and there she appealed, but in vain; she was sent about her dirty business.

"I'd help you if I could, Pansy, but there—I can't. So it's no good. I got children to keep, and if I gave you a job here you know what it'd be. I'd lose business. Sorry; but you're done. You're down and out, me gel."

She was. And when she realised that, tenser and colder became the desire to kill Tai Fu. She did not die. She did not wish to die. She did not dissolve in self-pity. It was a quieter business; the canker of the soul. She met a girl who had sometimes been to the Cocoa Rooms, and who was, indeed, watching for her, having heard the story. This friend gave her frocks and things and lessons in the art of man-leading, and Pansy began to grow and to live well, and to have money. Before her mother's grave was lit with the cheap red clovers, the daughter was known to fifty boys and many strange beds. But never once did her great desire fade or fail. She would kill Tai Fu; if not now, then at some good time that should appear.

*   *   *

It was the day of the Feast of the New Year, the mid-January celebrations in which Limehouse lives deliriously for some thirty hours. Pennyfields, the Causeway and West India Dock Road were whipped to stormy life with decorations. The windows shook with flowers. The roofs laughed with flags. Lanterns were looped from house to house, and ran from roof to post in a frenzy of Oriental colour and movement.

In the morning there was the solemn procession with joss-sticks to the cemetery, where prayers were held over the graves of the Chinese, and lamentations were carried out in native fashion—with sweet cakes, and whisky, and wine, and other delectables, also with song and gesture and dance.

In the evening—ah!—dancing in the halls with the girls. The glamorous January evening of Chinatown—yellow men, with much money to spend—beribboned, white girls, gay, flaunting and fond of curious kisses—rainbow lanterns, now lit, and swaying lithely on their strings—noise, bustle and laughter of the cafés—mad waste of food and drink—all these things touch the affair with an alluring quality of dream. Surely the girls may be forgiven if they love on such a night and with such people. Surely the sad lights of the Scandinavian Seamen's Home can have little attraction at an hour like this!

Of course, Pansy was there. She was known now. She was expected. Not by Tai Fu. With him she had had no dealings since the one night of horror she had spent under his roof. But tonight, in the gay confusion of the Causeway, she came suddenly and accidentally against his fat, greasy figure. She had apparently been jerked off her feet, and fell against his brown coat. He caught her. She looked up and, although on many occasions when he had invited her with a look in the street she had always killed him with a lip, she laughed.

"Ullo, Chinky dear! Fancy falling into your funny arms!"

He ambled, and smiled grotesquely. A small crowd, with fevered feet, mad for the hour, jostled and danced against them; and suddenly Pansy caught an outstretched yellow hand in one of hers, and, with the other circled about Tai Fu's waist, commenced to pull the bunch of them round in a whirligig.

The others caught the spirit of it, and round and round they went, till Pansy, in a hysterical exhaustion, dropped out, and collapsed in high laughter against a shop. Tai Fu, his pulses hot for her again, dropped out, too, and moved to her side. The others slacked off in a scuffle, and one, noting Tai Fu, who was the richest of them still, cried in Cantonese that he should invite them in and play host. In a shrill metallic voice, Pansy seconded it, grabbed Tai Fu's arm and bullied him into acceptance; and soon they were crowding to his upper room. The word went round that it was open doors at Tai Fu's, and soon half the Causeway was struggling into one small room, snatching food and drink.

On the way up the stairs Pansy leaned heavily against Tai Fu, sidling, nestling, and whispering words which he could not catch, but which sounded very sweet. He had his guests seated and bade them order from the restaurant waiter who had followed whatever they should require. Meantime, he squatted on a cane mat and drew Pansy to the cushions beside him; and there they sat, locked in one another's arms, her curls on his yellow neck, her skirts about his feet in a froth of petticoat lace.

The fun lasted for hours. It seemed impossible to tire the company.

Were they not feasting at the expense of Tai Fu, the miserly? But an Oriental revelry of the cheaper kind is a deadly affair, and Pansy found it so. The narcotised temperaments of the East, so blunted to joy or sorrow, catch a responsive note only from the loud and the barbaric. The solemn smokes swirled about the low room, and as it grew warmer and thicker, so did the faces grow moister and more pallid, so did the sense of smell grow sharper, and so did the bitter nightmare, brooding over the whole place, take hold on Pansy.

Tai Fu was drinking whisky, but Pansy only sipped tea. Her face, too, was pale and damp, but in that crowd, though now seared and world-weary, she was a wild rose. Suddenly she leaned heavily on her lover's arm, her chin uptilted to him. He was staring stupidly across the lanterned apartment. But the gay insouciance of Pansy recalled him, as she lolled backward, for he gave a sudden start and a clipped exclamation.

She was frolicsome tonight. "What's the matter, old dear?" she asked. "Found a pin? A-ah—naughty. Can't cuddle English girls without finding a pin, somewhere, Fuey dear. No rose without a thorn!"

She languished against him, and this time he withdrew his arm, and fingered her neck with his long hand, smiling idiotically. She pulled a bottle across the floor and filled his glass. He drank to her and, as a fiddler, with a one-stringed instrument, started a crooning accompaniment, he struggled up and would have her dance. He tried to help her, but fell, a little heavily, and Pansy fell over him, and there they rolled, to the joy of the company. Then Pansy scrambled up and danced.

It was a *danse macabre*. In that evil-smelling room, with those secret faces peering at her through the reeking smoke, she felt sick with the wine and the tumult; but her lips laughed, and she danced merrily, and Tai Fu sprawled and declared that she was a lovely girl.

The music stopped. Pansy stopped dancing and swooned in a seductive exhaustion into his big arms.

"Oh—damn—the—pins!" he said, picking each English word with care, while he dragged Pansy closer and sprawled over the cushions. He drank more whisky, and again good humour prevailed, and had Pansy heard the comments that were made about her she would, in spite of her profession, have shrivelled.

Now Tai Fu's hands became more familiar, and Pansy sportively rebuked him with an assumption of shocked virtue. He messed his fingers in her hair and drew her closer, pricking his arm with every embrace, while she reminded him that if you play with a bee you sometimes find the sting.

But he was by now too drunk to feel mere pin-pricks, and he rolled his great carcass about with languid laughter.

Later, he drank more whisky, and then began to look sick. He even excused himself, as feeling faint, and got up. Pansy clung to him.

"Don't go, old boy. Here—listen—don't send me away hungry. Aren't we going to have a little . . . love, eh, dearie?"

But he thrust her off. His jaw hung. He looked incipiently bilious. And suddenly he waved the company aside, and they, seeing that the show was at an end, straggled out, noisily and slowly. Pansy moved to him at the last, but it was certain that he was too sick for amusement, and he toddled with a friend to another room.

Pansy, left alone, went down the stairs and out into the clear, cold air and the midnight glitter of Poplar.

Tai Fu died that night of aconite poisoning. However, he had chewed strange leaves and preparations of leaves for so long that no one was much surprised. Certainly Pansy was not. When she heard of it, she murmured, "Oh!" airily, as though to say: "Damn good riddance."

For when she had undressed in her bedroom, on the night of the feast, she had removed from the belt of her waist a fine needle, which had lain for forty-eight hours in a distillation of aconite.

THE BIRD

IT is a tale that they tell softly in Pennyfields, when the curtains are drawn and the shapes of the night shut out. . . . Those who held that Captain Chudder, S.S. *Peacock*, owners, Peter Dubbin & Co., had a devil in him, were justified. But they were nearer the truth who held that his devil was not within him, but at his side, perching at his elbow, dropping sardonic utterance in his ear; moving with him day and night and prompting him—so it was held—to frightful excesses. His devil wore the shape of a white parrot, a bird of lusty wings and the cruellest of beaks. There were those who whispered that the old man had not always been the man that his crew knew him to be: that he had been a normal, kindly fellow until he acquired his strange companion from a native dealer in the malevolent Solomons. Certainly his maniac moods dated from its purchase; and there was truth in the dark hints of his men that there was something wrong with that damned bird . . . a kind of . . . something you sort of felt when it looked at you or answered you back. For one thing, it had a diabolical knack of mimicry, and many a chap would cry: "Yes, George!" or "Right, sir!" in answer to a commanding voice which chuckled with glee as he came smartly to order. They invariably referred to it as "that bloody bird," though actually it had done nothing to merit such opprobrium. When they thought it over calmly, they could think of no harm that it had done to them: nothing to arouse such loathing as every man on the boat felt towards it. It was not spiteful; it was not bad-tempered. Mostly it was in cheery mood and would chuckle deep in the throat, like the Captain, and echo or answer, quite pleasantly, such remarks, usually rude, as were addressed to it.

And yet . . . Somehow . . .

There it was. It was always there—everywhere; and in its speech they seemed to find a sinister tone which left them guessing at the meaning of its words. On one occasion, the cook, in the seclusion of the fo'c'sle, had remarked that he would like to wring its neck if he could get hold of it; but old grizzled Snorter had replied that that bird couldn't be killed. There was a something about that bird that . . . well, he betted no one wouldn't touch that bird without trouble. And a moment of panic stabbed the crowd as a voice leapt from the sombre shadows of the corner:

"That's the style, me old brown son. Don't try to come it with me—what?" and ceased on a spasmodic flutter of wicked white wings.

That night, as the cook was ascending the companion, he was caught by a huge sea, which swept across the boat from nowhere and dashed him, head-on, below. For a week he was sick with a broken head, and throughout that week the bird would thrust its beak to the berth where he lay, and chortle to him:

"Yep, me old brown son. Wring his bleeding neck—what? Waltz me around again, Willie, round and round and round!"

That is the seamen's story and, as the air of Limehouse is thick with seamen's stories, it is not always good to believe them. But it is a widely known fact that on his last voyage the Captain did have a devil with him, the foulest of all devils that possess mortal men: not the devil of slaughter, but the devil of cruelty. They were from Swatow to London, and it was noted that he was drinking heavily ashore, and he continued the game throughout the voyage. home dot hiwaay dot net backslash tilde ajohns backslash retro backslash Etext dot htm. He came aboard from Swatow, drunk, bringing with him a Chinese boy, also drunk. The greaser, being a big man, kicked him below; otherwise, the boat in his charge would have gone there; and so he sat or sprawled in his cabin, with a rum bottle before him and, on the corner of his chair, the white parrot, which conversed with him and sometimes fluttered on deck to shout orders in the frightful voice of his master and chuckle to see them momentarily obeyed.

"Yes," repeated old man Snorter, sententiously, "I'd run a hundred miles 'fore I'd try to monkey with the old man or his bloody bird. There's something about that bird. . . . I said so before. I 'eard a story once about a bird. Out in T'aip'ing I 'eard it. It'll make yeh sick if I tell it. . . ."

Now while the Captain remained drunk in his cabin, he kept with him for company the miserable, half-starved Chinky boy whom he had brought aboard. And it would make others sick if the full dark tale were told here of what the master of the *Peacock* did to that boy. You may read of monstrosities in police reports of cruelty cases; you may read old records of the Middle Ages; but the bestialities of Captain Chudder could not be told in words.

His orgy of drink and delicious torture lasted till they were berthed in the Thames; and the details remain sharp and clear in the memories of those who witnessed it. At all the ceremonial horrors which were wrought in that wretched cabin, the parrot was present. It jabbered to the old man; the old man jabbered back, and gave it an occasional sip of rum from his glass; and the parrot would mimic the Chink's entreaties, and wag a grave claw at him as he writhed under the ritual of punishment; and when that day's ceremony was finished it would flutter from bow to stern of the boat, its cadaverous figure stinging the shadows with shapes of fear for all aboard; perching here, perching there, simpering and whining in tune with the Chink's placid moaning.

Placid; yes, outwardly. But the old man's wickedness had lighted a flame beneath that yellow skin which nothing could quench: nothing but the floods of vengeance. Had the old man been a little more cute and a little less drunk, he might have remembered that a Chinaman does not forget. He would have read danger in the face that was so submissive under his devilries. Perhaps he did see it, but, because of the rum that was in him, felt himself secure from the hate of any outcast Chink; knew that his victim would never once get the chance to repay him, Captain Chudder, master of the *Peacock*, and one of the very smartest. The Chink was alone and weaponless, and dare not come aft without orders. He was master of the boat; he had a crew to help him, and knives and guns, and he had his faithful white bird to warn him. Too, as soon as they docked at Limehouse, he would sling him off or arrange quick transfer to an outward boat, since he had no further use for him.

But it happened that he made no attempt to transfer. He had forgotten that idea. He just sat below, finished his last two bottles, paid off his men, and then, after a sleep, went ashore to report. Having done that, he forgot all trivial affairs, such as business, and set himself seriously to search for amusement. He climbed St. George's, planning a real good old booze-up, and the prospect that spread itself before his mind was so compelling that he did not notice a lurking yellow phantom that hung on his shadow. He visited the Baltic on the chance of finding an old pal or so, and, meeting none, he called at a shipping office at Fenchurch Street, where he picked up an acquaintance, and they two returned eastward to Poplar, and the phantom feet *sup-supped* after them. Through the maze and clamour of the London streets and traffic the shadow slid; it dodged and danced about the Captain's little cottage in Gill Street; and when he, and others, came out and strolled to a bar, and, later, to a music hall, it flitted, mothlike, around them.

Surely, since there is no step in the world that has just the obvious stealth of the Chinaman's, he must have heard those whispering feet? Surely his path was darkened by that shadow? But no. After the music hall he drifted to a waterside wineshop, and then, with a bunch of the others, went wandering.

It was late. Eleven notes straggled across the waters from many grey towers. Sirens were screeching their derisive song; and names of various Scotch whiskies spelt themselves in letters of yellow flame along the night. Far in the darkness a voice was giving the chanty:

"What shall we do with a drunken sailor?"

The Captain braced himself up and promised himself a real glittering night of good-fellowship, and from gin-warmed bar to gin-warmed bar he roved, meeting the lurid girls of the places and taking one of them upstairs. At the last bar his friends, too, went upstairs with their ladies, and, it being then one o'clock in the morning, he brought a pleasant evening to a close at a certain house in Poplar High Street, where he took an hour's amusement by flinging half-crowns over the fan-tan table.

But always the yellow moth was near, and when, at half-past two, he came, with uncertain step, into the sad street, now darkened and loud only with the drunken, who found unfamiliar turnings in familiar streets, and old landmarks many yards away from their rightful places, the moth buzzed closer and closer.

The Captain talked as he went. He talked of the night he had had, and the girls his hands had touched. His hard face was cracked to a meaningless smile, and he spat words at obstructive lampposts and kerbstones, and swears dropped like toads from his lips. But at last he found his haven in Gill Street, and his hefty brother, with whom he lived when ashore, shoved him upstairs to his bedroom. He fell across the bed, and the sleep of the swinish held him fast.

*   *   *

The grey towers were tolling three o'clock, and the thick darkness of the waterside covered the night like a blanket. The lamps were pale and few. The waters slucked miserably at the staples of the wharves. One heard the measured beat of a constable's boot; sometimes the rattle of chains and blocks; mournful hooters; shudders of noise as engines butted lines of trucks at the shunting station.

Captain Chudder slept, breathing stertorously, mouth open, limbs heavy and nerveless. His room was deeply dark, and so little light shone on the back reaches of the Gill Street cottages that the soft raising of the window made no visible aperture. Into this blank space something rose from below, and soon it took the shape of a flat, yellow face which hung motionless, peering into the room. Then a yellow hand came through; the aperture was widened; and swiftly and silently a lithe, yellow body hauled itself up and slipped over the sill.

It glided, with outstretched hand, from the window, and, the moment it touched the bed, its feeling fingers went here and there, and it stood still, gazing upon the sleep of drunkenness. Calmly and methodically a yellow hand moved to its waist and withdrew a kreese. The same hand raised the kreese and held it poised. It was long, keen and beautifully curved, but not a ray of light was in the room to fall upon it, and the yellow hand had to feel its bright blade to find whether the curve ran from or towards it.

Then, with terrific force and speed, it came down: one—two—three. The last breath rushed from the open lips. Captain Chudder was out.

The strong yellow hand withdrew the kreese for the last time, wiped it on the coverlet of the bed, and replaced it in its home. The figure turned, like a wraith, for the window; turned for the window and found, in a moment of panic, that it knew not which way to turn. It hesitated a moment. It thought it heard a sound at the bed. It touched the coverlet and the boots of the Captain; all was still. Stretching a hand to the wall, Sung Dee began to creep and to feel his way along. Dark as the room was, he had found his way in, without matches or illuminant. Why could he not find his way out? Why was he afraid of something?

Blank wall was all he found at first. Then his hand touched what seemed to be a picture frame. It swung and clicked and the noise seemed to echo through the still house. He moved farther, and a sharp rattle told him that he had struck the loose handle of the door. But that was of little help. He could not use the door; he knew not what perils lay behind it. It was the window he wanted—the window.

Again he heard that sound from the bed. He stepped boldly forward and judged that he was standing in the middle of the room. Momentarily a sharp shock surged over him. He prayed for matches, and something in his throat was almost crying: "The window! The window!" He seemed like an island in a sea of darkness; one man surrounded by legions of immortal, intangible enemies. His cold Chinese heart went hot with fear.

The middle of the room, he judged, and took another step forward, a step which landed his chin sharply against the jutting edge of the mantel-shelf over the fireplace. He jumped like a cat and his limbs shook; for now he had lost the door and the bed, as well as the window, and had made terrible noises which might bring disaster. All sense of direction was gone. He knew not whether to go forward or backward, to right or left.

He heard the tinkle of the shunting trains, and he heard a rich voice crying something in his own tongue. But he was lapped around by darkness and terror, and a cruel fancy came to him that he was imprisoned here for ever and for ever, and that he would never escape from this enveloping, suffocating room. He began to think that—

And then a hot iron of agony rushed down his thick back as, sharp and clear at his elbow, came the Captain's voice:

"Get forrard, you damn lousy Chink—get forrard. Lively there! Get out of my room!"

He sprang madly aside from the voice that had been the terror of his life for so many weeks, and collided with the door; realised that he had made further fearful noises; dashed away from it and crashed into the bed; fell across it and across the warm, wet body that lay there. Every nerve in every limb of him was seared with horror at the contact, and he leapt off, kicking, biting, writhing. He leapt off, and fell against a table, which tottered, and at last fell with a stupendous crash into the fender.

"Lively, you damn Chink!" said the Captain. "Lively, I tell yeh. Dance, d'yeh hear? I'll have yeh for this. I'll learn you something. I'll give you something with a sharp knife and a bit of hot iron, my cocky. I'll make yer yellow skin crackle, yeh damn lousy chopstick. I'll have yeh in a minute. And when I get yeh, orf with yeh clothes. I'll cut yeh to pieces, I will."

Sung Dee shrieked. He ran round and round, beating the wall with his hands, laughing, crying, jumping, while all manner of shapes arose in his path, lit by the grey light of fear. He realised that it was all up now. He cared not how much noise he made. He hadn't killed the old man; only wounded him. And now all he desired was to find the door and any human creatures who might save him from the Captain. He met the bed again, suddenly, and the tormentor who lay there. He met the upturned table and fell upon it, and he met the fireplace and the blank wall; but never, never the window or the door. They had vanished. There was no way out. He was caught in that dark room, and the Captain would do as he liked with him. . . . He heard footsteps in the passage and sounds of menace and alarm below. But to him they were friendly sounds, and he screamed loudly toward them.

He cried to the Captain, in his pidgin, for mercy.

"Oh, Captain—no burn me today, Captain. Sung Dee be heap good sailor, heap good servant, all same slave. Sung Dee heap plenty solly hurt Captain. Sung Dee be good boy. No do feller bad lings no feller more. O Captain. Let Sung Dee go lis time. Let Sung Dee go. O Captain!"

But "Oh, my Gawd!" answered the Captain. "Bless your yellow heart. Wait till I get you trussed up. Wait till I get you below. I'll learn yeh."

And now those below came upstairs, and they listened in the passage, and for the space of a minute they were hesitant. For they heard all manner of terrible noises, and by the noises there might have been half-a-dozen fellows in the Captain's room. But very soon the screaming and the pattering feet were still, and they heard nothing but low moans; and at last the bravest of them, the Captain's brother, swung the door open and flashed a large lantern.

And those who were with him fell back in dumb horror, while the brother cried harshly: "Oh! . . . my . . . God!" For the lantern shone on a Chinaman seated on the edge of the bed. Across his knees lay the dead body of the Captain, and the Chink was fondling his damp, dead face, talking baby talk to him, dancing him on his knee, and now and then making idiot moans. But what sent the crowd back in horror was that a great death-white Thing was flapping about the yellow face of the Chink, cackling: "I'll learn yeh! I'll learn yeh!" and dragging strips of flesh away with every movement of the beak.

GINA OF THE CHINATOWN
A Reminiscence

MEMORY is a delicate instrument. Like an old musical box, it will lie silent for long years; then a mere nothing, a jerk, a tremor, will start the spring, and from beneath its decent covering of dust it will talk to us of forgotten passion and desire. Some memories are thus moved at sight of a ribbon, a faded violet, a hotel bill; others at the sound of a voice or a bar of music, or at the bite of a flavour on the palate or an arrangement of skies against a well-known background. To me return all the unhappy, far-off things when I smell the sharp odour of a little dirty theatre near Blackwall. Then I think upon all those essences of life most fragrant and fresh, and upon . . . Gina Bertello.

Gina Bertello was as facile and appealing as the syllables of her name. At thirteen she was the happiest and best-loved child in Acacia Grove, Poplar; for she had those three rare qualities which, together, will carry any pilgrim safely through this world to the higher blisses of the next: she was gentle—and brave—and gay.

You might then have seen her about the streets at all hours of day and night, a frail slip of a kiddie, delicate as a watercolour, swift and restless as a bird. From her little head hung twenty bright yellow curls, short to the neck, and these curls shook and caught the sun fifty times to the minute as she shot her sharp glances, which rested on nothing and yet reflected everything. Liquid fire seemed to run under the light skin, and the lines of her figure, every one of which had something true to say to you, were of an almost epigrammatic neatness. Small as she was, she was perfectly built, and dressed with that careful contempt for taste which you may observe in the attire of all children of theatrical parents. A black satin frock kissed the slim, stockinged leg at the delicately correct moment; a scarlet band held the waist; a scarlet hat crowned all; and the shock of short curls, chiming with the black and scarlet, made an unforgettable picture which always appealed to the stage sense of her old dad, Batty Bertello. Moreover, there; was the practical advantage that if ever you wanted your Gina in a hurry, when she was out playing, you could always pick her from any bunch of children half-a-mile away. Also, she could never be lost, for she stood alone. Indeed, no child has ever been seen, either in Poplar or in Kensington, of such arresting appearance as this rumple-headed darling who, for twelve months, flitted, in small type, across the bills of the minor music halls. She was as distinctive as a negro in a snowstorm; and when she was taken to theatres or concerts beyond the confines of Poplar where she was known, people turned to stare at her, and turned again to stare. There was about her some elfish quality that made her seem only half real. Even her old dad could not quite believe in her. He fully expected some morning to wake up and find that she had slipped away to the bluebell or daffodil from which she had escaped.

"That youngster of mine," he would say, "is hot stuff. She don't half get on. Come round next Sunday night, and we'll have some music. Y'ought to hear her play. Rachmaninoff prelude, *Valse Triste*, Mozart sonatas. Fairly tears the back hair off yeh. Got temperament, that kid. She's coming up, too, with her dancing. Oh, she's hot."

Mrs. Bertello would echo him, but a little sadly; for, as Gina grew, from seven to thirteen, so did Mrs. Bertello fade and fade and withdraw more and more upstage. Gina was going to get on; she knew it. She knew, too, that Gina would get on without any help from her; so she stood in the background and grew careless about herself and her person. She wore old clothes and old manners. She snuffled. She loafed about the house and in bed, and she let things go. If only she could have felt that the getting on of Gina depended upon her. . . . But by the time the child was seven she realised that she stood in the presence of something stronger than herself. It frightened and distressed her that she should have produced something so sharp and foreign. She knew that she was loved and always would be loved. But she wanted most of all to be wanted. And she wasn't.

At twelve Gina was running the home. Old dad was dresser to a red-nose bill-topper, which meant that he did not finish work until two o'clock in the morning. It was Gina who sat up every night to serve his supper, Mumdear toddled to bed with a little warm whisky, leaving Gina in the kitchen with queer books—Tennyson, Browning, Childe Harold, *Lives of the Composers*, *The Golden Treasury*, Marcus Aurelius, *The Faerie Queene*. At two o'clock old dad would bounce in, full of anecdote and reminiscence and original whimsy, and they would sup together, Gina, from the age of eleven, always taking a glass of beer and a cigarette with him. It was he who had bought her those books. It was he who had interested his guv'nor in the kid, so that the guv'nor had handed him money wherewith to get music lessons and to secure a practice piano. It was he who had spoken to Madame Gilibert, controller of the famous music-hall child-dancers, the Casino Juveniles; and Madame, recognising that dad was dresser to a star, and might, in certain underground ways, be useful, took the child and put her through a course. Within the first week she thought she had found a Taglioni, and that hers would be the honour—and the commission. Of course she hadn't found a Taglioni, and none knew that better than Gina, though she did not say so, for she believed in taking what we can while we can.

It was old dad, too, who had made a companion of her and talked to her, through those late hours, of the things that could be done in the world—of the things that he himself had tried and failed to do. He had talked to her of laughter and courage and endurance, and of "playing the game."

From him she had inherited a love of all raw and simple things, all that was odorous of the flesh. She hated country solitudes, and she loved Poplar and the lights and the noise of people. She loved it for its blatant life. She loved the streets, the glamour, the diamond dusks, the dirt and the perfume. She loved the shops and the stalls, with their alluring treasures—treasures, moreover, that you could buy, not, as in the West, priced beyond your maddest dreams. There was Salmon Lane market. There were the docks. There were the fearsome Malays. There was the Chinese quarter. There was the Isle of Dogs, with its exciting bridges and waterways. There were the timid twilights and the homecomings; the merry boys and girls of the pavements, and the softly lighted windows. She loved them all, and they became all part of her; and she was right in loving them. For Poplar is a land of homes, and where a thousand homes are gathered together, there do we find beauty and prayer. There, among the ashpits and broken boats and dry canals, are girls and garlands and all the old, lovely things that help the human heart to float along its winding courses to the sea. The shapes, sounds, colours and silences of the place shook her to wonder, and the flamboyant curves of the road to Barking, where are lean grey streets of villas and vociferant markets, were always to her the way to the Realms of Gold. Every street was a sharp-flavoured adventure, and at night each had a little untranslatable message for her. Everywhere she built romances. She was a mandarin's daughter in Pennyfields. She was a sailor's wife in the Isle of Dogs. In the West India Dock Road she was a South Sea princess, decked with barbaric jewels and very terrible knives. She did not like western London: it wasn't homey. She loved only the common joys of the flesh and the common joys of the heart; and these she found in Poplar. It was all so cosy and sweet and—oh, everything that you couldn't talk about. The simple mateyness of it all sometimes made her cry. It made her cry because she wanted to tell someone about it; and she couldn't—until . . . a year later . . . she began to dance. Then she told everything.

In the Chinatown Causeway, too, were half-tones of rose and silver, stately moving cutthroats, up from the great green Pacific, and the muffled wail of reed instruments in a song last heard in Formosa. Cinnamon and aconite, betel and bhang hung on the air. There was the blue moon of the Orient. There, for the bold, were the sharp knives, and there, for those who would patiently seek, was the lamp of young Aladdin. I think Gina must have found it.

She loved Poplar, and, loving so, she commanded love, as you will learn if you inquire concerning her. When she danced it was Poplar that she expressed, and Poplar worshipped her for it.

At twelve years old she was dismissed from the local Board School for the sound reason that the teachers confessed their inability to teach her anything more. She was too sharp for them. Her morality she summed up in answer to a teacher's question as to what she understood by religion.

"I believe in enjoying yourself, dears, and enjoying other people as well, and making them enjoy you."

That was her creed, and as to her adherence to it and the efficacy of it you must ask the people of Acacia Grove and thereabouts. Old dad shrugged his shoulders, and in the saloon of the Blue Lantern he explained:

"Ah—when you've got anything as hot as our Gina, it don't do to try and learn 'em things. You can't. They knew it all centuries before you was born. And what they don't know they'll find out without bothering anyone. Give 'em their heads—that's all you can do with that kind of kid. Stand aside; she'll develop herself."

Gina was thirteen years and six months when news was brought one morning to the narrow fastnesses of Acacia Grove that old dad had been killed in a street accident. At that moment she was standing at the gate nursing Philip, the next-door baby.

She stared. She caught her breath as from a sharp blow. Her face was, for the first and only time in her life, expressionless. Then, with a matter-of-fact movement, she deposited Philip on the cold kerb, looked up, addressed the eternities, and for one minute told God, in good set terms, exactly what she thought about Him. When thus relieved, she shrugged her little shoulders and gathered up the baby.

"Ah, well. Hearts are trumps. Globe Polish is the best. The Lord Mayor's coachman says so, Philip of Macedon. Looks from here, Philip of

Macedon, as though I'd have to get busy."

A week after the funeral, she stood in her dingy bedroom, and posed herself before the mirror with a graceful egotism. The slender stockinged legs looked that morning singularly pert and self-sufficient. The black satin jacket had an air of past adventure amid large things. She adjusted the black lace hat the tiniest shade to the left of the luscious curls, and nodded.

"Well. Something's got to be done, and if I don't do it no one else will. Don't believe in waiting for your ship to come in. Only thing to do is to get a bally boat and row out to meet it. Laugh and the world laughs with you. Weep and you'll get a red nose, Gina, my darling. Now off we go to make ourselves as welcome as a snowflake in hell."

An hour later she was a member of the Casino Juveniles, under the direction of Madame Gilibert, and three hours later was hard at work rehearsing.

Many folk of Poplar must have experienced only a mixed sorrow at the sudden end of Batty Bertello. For if the old dad had not gone out so suddenly Gina would never have been forced to start work to support Mumdear; and had she not started just at that moment, she would never have become a public character; and in that event we should have lost—what should we have lost?

Well, everything that in those days made life worth living. For it was Gina, that mop-haired, fragile baby, who taught thousands of us how to live.

And her beginnings as a public character were in this wise.

The turn of the Casino Juveniles consisted of vocal *soli*, concerted numbers, *pas seuls*, and ensembles, in the costumes of the early nineteenth century. It was entitled *Old-fashioned Flowers* (you may remember it), and, with a nice catholicity, it embraced the minuet and the pavane no less than the latest coon song and dance. At the end of the first show, Madame expressed herself as well satisfied with Gina.

"Seems to have a real—what you might call flare—for the stage. Understands what she's doing. Made for a dancer. Let's hope she don't grow."

For the tragedy of the good lady's life was that her children would grow, and every two years or so they had to be weeded out and new little girls laboriously trained to take the places of those who possessed neither the divine grace of the juvenile nor the selfassurance of the adult. She had a much-furrowed face, and swore hybrid oaths at electricians and stage hands. They understood.

For the first week, Gina thoroughly enjoyed herself, and, true to her creed, forced the rest of the company to enjoy her.

Sharp at five every afternoon, she had to appear at the centre where the private omnibus collected the children and whisked them away to the first hall, where they were an early number—on at seven-five—for the first house. Then, out of that hall to another at the far side of London, where they were a concluding number for the first house. Then back to the starting-place for the second house, and off again to finish at the distant hall. At about one in the morning she would trip home to supper, which Mumdear left in the kitchen oven. So to bed. At ten o'clock next morning Mumdear would bring her a cup of tea and a cigarette, and at about noon she would descend, unless a rehearsal were called for eleven.

Then, one brave night, came her chance to display that Ginaesque quality that made her loved and admired by all who knew her. In a low riverside hall in the Blackball direction the Casino Juveniles were the bill-footers. This hall was a relic of the old times and the old manners—a plaintive echo of the days when the music hall was little more than a cave of harmony, with a sawdusted floor, a husky waiter, and a bull-throated chairman. Efforts to bring it up to date by renovation and structural alteration had only had the effect of emphasising its age, and its threepenny gallery and its fourpenny pit told their own tale.

By this time Gina had, by some subtle means, unknown to herself or to others, established herself as leader of the Casinos. Her compelling personality, her wide knowledge of "things" as well as matters of general interest, and her confident sagacity, had, together, drawn even those youngsters who had been two years with the turn to look to her as a final court of appeal in all questions and disputes. They listened to her ideas of dance, and took cues from her that rightly should have come from the titular leader. Perhaps it was the touch of devil which alternately smouldered and flamed in Gina's eyes that was the real secret of her domination of her fellows; a touch that came from the splash of soft Southern blood in her veins, bequeathed by a grandfather who, in his early twenties, mislaid his clasp-knife somewhere between the ribs of a neighbour on the island of Sicily, and found it expedient to give up the search for it and come to England. This languorous, sun-loved blood, fused with the steady blood of the North, resulted in a mixture which raced under her skin with the passion and energy of a greyhound, and gave her that mysterious élan which decided, as soon as she could walk, that she was born for dance.

On the big night—a Wednesday: early-closing night—the hall was playing to good business. It was lit with a suave brilliance. Gallery packed, pit packed, stalls packed, and the gangway by the babbling bar packed close with the lads of the waterside—blacks, white toughs, and yellow men.

The air was mephitic: loud with foot and voice and glass. It stunk of snarling song. Solemn smokes of cut plug swirled in a haze of lilac up to the dreary rim of gallery and the chimera of corpse faces that swam above it. At nine-ten Gina and the rest of the Casinos stood in the wings, watching the turn that preceded them on the bill—Luigi Cadenza, the world-renowned Italian tenor: salary three guineas per week for thirteen shows a week—who was handing *Santa Lucia* and *O sole mio* to an indifferent audience; for in vaudeville it is the early turn that gets the bird. Near them stood the manager, discussing the Lincolnshire probables with the stage manager. Much dirty and faded scenery, alleged fireproof, was piled to the flies, and on either side were iron doors and stone staircases. Everywhere were strong draughts and crusted dirt.

Suddenly, from behind a sweep of canvas, leapt an antic figure, dishevelled, begrimed, inarticulate. It plucked the manager by the sleeve.

"Wire's fused, sir. Caught oner the flies. Blazing like old hell."

The manager jerked his neck at the stage manager.

"Ring down!"

A bell tinkled, and the shabby purple curtain dropped on the world-renowned tenor in the midst of his *Santa Luci-i-i-a,* and smothered him with confusion and with its own folds.

The neck jerked again.

"Ring down safety, too."

He shot a hand to the telephone, rang through to the orchestra and spoke two words.

The conductor in front saw the flash of the light at his desk. He bent to the receiver. Two words snapped from it: *The King.* He replaced the receiver. His baton fell, and the symphony of *Santa Lucia* dribbled away to rubbish. He mouthed at his leader: *The King.* He rose in his chair and tapped; and the band blared the first bar of the National Anthem when again the bell tinkled. Again he snatched the receiver: "Cut *The King,*" snapped a blasphemous voice. "Keep going on Cadenza."

Behind, things were happening.

"Where's that damn 'lectrician?" The manager appealed, exhorted and condemned. The electrician, having carried the bad news, had vanished; but the typhoon of language whirled him back again.

"'Sail right, guv'nor. 'Sail right now. We got it under. You can ring up again."

But it was too late. The sudden dropping of the curtain, the incipient glide and recovery of the safety, the cessation and hurried resumption of the music, had disturbed the house. There were sounds of many moving feet, an uneasy rustle, as when a multitude of people begin to pull themselves together. Then the inevitable fool made the fool's remark.

"There's something wrong somewhere. *Fire*, shouldn't wonder."

That word did it.

The house rose to its feet. It swayed in two vast presses to right and left. A woman screamed. Feet scraped and stamped. The chuckers-out bawled:

"Order, there. Kepp yeh seats, cancher! Nothing ain't wrong!"

The conductor rose and faced the house.

"Resume your seats, *please*. There's no danger of any kind. The band will now play *Hiawatha*. Give 'em a few chords!" he called to his brass and drums, and half-a-dozen tantararas drowned the noise of the struggles and counter-struggles of those who would go and those who would urge them to stay.

A panicky stripling, seeing a clear way, vaulted the partition between pit and stalls, and was promptly floored by one on the jaw from Hercules in uniform. He howled. Stalls struggled to see him, and the pit pushed the stalls back. Many women screamed. They were carried out, kicking. Men told other men that there was nothing the matter. They clambered on seats to say it. They struck with fist and boot other men who disagreed with them. The yellow and black men dashed hither and thither, receiving many blows but never ceasing to run. They did not know for what or from what they ran. They ran because they ran. A group of lads raided the bar. They helped themselves and they smashed many glasses and bottles. The chuckers-out became oathful and malevolent. They hit right and left.

In the wings, the manager was dumb. His mouth had vomited the entire black vocabulary. He had nothing more to say. The skirts of his dress coat had the appearance of two exhausted tongues. The position of his tie showed that he was a man smitten and afflicted: one who had attempted large things while knowing himself to lack the force necessary to achieve them; one who had climbed the steeps of pain to the bally limit; one who was no longer a man but a tortured organism.

"Billie," he cried to the red-nose bill-topper, "Billie, for Christ's sake go on, and quiet 'em, there's a good chap. This is the sack for me, if there's a panic."

"No good, old boy. Sorry. Can't do anything with a mixed gang like yours. Nearly got the blasted bird just now."

"Well—you—Miss Gutacre. For the Lord's sake—go on. Give 'em any-thing. Give 'em *He tickled the Lady's Fancy*."

"Oh, Jack, old man, I daren't," whimpered the stout soubrette. "I couldn't hold 'em. I've never faced a gang like that. If Billie won't go, I won't. 'Tain't fair to ask me."

"Well, you're a couple of damn devils, that's what you are—I beg pardon—I mean. No, but, look here. . . . If—"

He broke off, suddenly aware that someone was peremptorily agi-tating his coattails.

"What the blazes d'you want, kid?"

"I'll go on, sir," said Gina placidly.

"You? What the heaven d'you think a shrimp like you can do?"

"I can hold 'em, sir. I know I can. Bet you what you like. Turn me loose, and see! Ring the orchestra for *La Maxixe*, one verse and dance."

"Mr. Catanach!" A boy in a disordered uniform sprang from nowhere. "You're wanted here—quick."

The manager swung four ways at once, unable to go one way for thought of the others. Then he gave two orders to the stage manager.

"Ring through for the *Masheesh*. Then send that kid on."

Gina was one of those delightful people who believe in impulse rather than in consideration. What she had proposed to the manager was an impulse of the moment; it simply didn't bear thinking about. She could hear the complaints, loud and cruel, of that brute which she had under-taken to tame—she heard scream and roar; stamp of nailed feet; fury of blow against blow; temper against temper; the fall of glass; the wail of the victim, the howl of the aggressor.

But now, through the clamour, there came to her, faint and sweet and far away, the ecstatic wail of *La Maxixe*, swelling insistently as the curtain swung up. The first bars settled her fears. The music stole into her blood and possessed every nerve and tissue of her eager little body. It was in her feet and her hands and her heart. The stage manager gave her a gentle shove.

"Get on, Kiddie. You got a rotten rough house. Good luck."

With a toss of her yellow head and a stamp of impetuous feet she dashed on. Along the stage she charged, in animal grace and bravery, once, twice, with loose heel dancing, and noted with approval that the clamour was a little less in volume and that many faces were turned to the stage to look at this small figure, immature yet cunningly finished. With as much clatter as her furious little shoes would produce, she ran to the back-cloth. The dust rose in answering clouds and was blown into the auditorium, where it mingled with the opiate haze and was duly swallowed by the gaping ones. The music surged over the footlights in a compelling flood. The *chef d'orchestre* had caught the idea, and she could see that he was helping her. The fiddles tossed it to her in a tempest of bows, the brass and woodwind blared it in a tornado, the drum insisted on it, and, like a breaker, it seemed to rise up to her. Before her opened a cavern of purple, stung with sharp lamps in the distant dusks. It swayed and growled and seemed to open a horrid mouth. But between her and it, she thanked her Heavenly Father, was the music, a little pool of dream, flinging its spray upon her. The stage seemed drenched in it and, seizing the tactful moment, she raced down to the footlights and flung herself into it, caressing and caressed by it, shaking, as it were, little showers of sound from her delighted limbs.

Every phrase of its wistful message was reflected in that marvellously expressive form, rosy and slender and taut. You would have said that each pulse of her body was singing for joy of it, and when her light voice picked up the melody with:

> *"Oh, meet me in the Val-ley*
> *The hap-py Val-ley,"*

interpolated with back-chat to the front rows of the stalls, there was a movement towards repose and attention to this appealing picture.

"Come on, Charl, while there's a chance, case there's a fire."

"No; 'alf a mo', Perce. Ain't no fire. I'm going to watch this. Looks like being funny. Got some pluck, y'know, that youngster."

She stamped along the stage in a cloud of lace and tossing frock; then, seeing that they were still moving and, in the far reaches, struggling, she loosened her heel and suddenly—off went one shoe to the wings, prompt side. Off went the other to the wings, o.p. This bit of business attracted the attention of Charl and Perce and others. They closed in. Now it was heel-and-toe dancing, and suddenly a small hand shot to her knee. Off came a little crimson garter. With an airy turn of her bare and white-powdered arm she sent it spinning into the stalls. "Scramble for it, darlings!"

> *"I'll—tell—you—how I love you—*
> *Down in the Valley."*

The wicked little head ogled, now here, now there.

They scrambled, and while they scrambled and she danced, she bent to her right knee, and off came a blue garter, and away that went, too.

"Share and share alike, old dears."

This time she had the pit as well.

"My word. She's a corker, eh?"

"I should say so."

"Quite right, Augustus," she cried. "There isn't a fire here, but I'm hot enough to start one. I love my molten lava, but what price Gina?"

They chuckled. They cheered. They chi-iked.

"Gaw—fancy a kid like that. . . . If she was a kid of mine I'd learn 'er something."

In the vaudeville phrase, she had got 'em with both hands.

The lights died down again. The turmoil was confined to the gallery. A lone chucker-out implored them to observe that everything was all right and "Order, please, for the artiste." The Maxixe swallowed him up.

"Come along, boys!" cried Gina. "Chorus, this time. Now then—one—two—

> *"I'll . . .*
> *Meet . . . You . . .*
> *In . . .*
> *the Valley . . ."*

Very uncertainly and timidly a few at the back of the hall picked it up. They hummed it in the selfconscious voice of the music-hall audience before it is certain that it is not alone. The next few lines were taken with more confidence, and by those in front as well, and the last lines, encouraged by the band and the shrill abandon of Gina, they yelled defiantly, exultingly, with whistles and cheers for the kid.

Those standing up were pressed forward as those behind strove to catch her back-chat with stalls and orchestra.

"Holler, boys," she cried, shaking her dusty golden head from side to side. "Holler! All together—tenors—basses—Worthingtons. More you holler the more money I get. And if I don't take some home to my old man tonight I shall get it where Susie wore the beads! Holler, boys: it's my benefit! Edison-Bell record!"

And they did holler. Away they went in one broad roar. There was no doubt as to whether Gina had fulfilled her promise of holding them. There was no doubt as to whether she had a stage personality. That holler settled it. Gina's vocation lay in the stress and sacrifice of the vulgar world.

"My word, she's a little goer, eh?"

"You're right. At that age, too! Fast little cat. She wants a spanking. And if she was a kid o' mine she'd get it."

"How old is she?"

"Fourteen, they say."

"Lord, she'll be a corker in a year or two's time."

"Year or two's time. Hot stuff now if you ask me."

Perhaps she was. But she had saved the situation. She had averted a panic. She had saved the loss of life inseparable from a theatre stampede. And she knew it. As the audience settled down to be amused by her, or by the next turn for whom she had prepared the way, she gave the conductor the cue for the coda, and, with a final stamp of those inspired feet, she leapt into the wings, where the rest of the Casinos awaited her. She was gasping, with drawn face. Two light blue stockings, robbed of their garters, were slipping halfway down her delicately rounded legs. The dust from the stage had gathered on her warm arms. She was plainly "all gone." But there was a light in her eye and that in her manner that shrieked: "What did I tell you?"

The manager came to meet her.

"You glorious kid!"

Pertly she looked up at him.

"Yes, ain't I? Going to push a boat out for me?"

"Push a boat out?"

"Yes; I'm dry after that. Mine's a claret and soda."

He rumpled his hair to bring it into keeping with his unhappy evening-clothes. He gestured operatically. He embraced the universe. He addressed the eternal verities.

"I'm damned," he exclaimed, "I'm damned if I don't book that kid for six months."

*   *   *

He kept his promise. She was booked at three pounds per week for six months, and she thought she was in heaven. She had never dreamed that there was so much money in the world. Then there was a hurrying to and fro in Acacia Grove. She had to work up an act of her own and provide her own makeup box and dresses. In the former she was assisted by Madame Gilibert and the *chef d'orchestre*; in the latter by Mumdear and the whole female population of Acacia Grove. Band parts had to be arranged and collected, each instrumental part secured in a neat stiff cover, engraved in gilt letters:

GINA
Piccolo

and

GINA
Cornet

Madame Gilibert sent invitation cards to all managers, and even booked one of the inch-square spaces on the back cover of The Encore, where Gina's picture duly appeared:

GINA
The Marvellous Child Dancer
The Pocket Kate Vaughan
All com. Gilibert.

amid that bewildering array of faces which makes the cover of that journal so distinctive on the bookstall and so deeply interesting to the student of physiognomy and of human nature. So she started as a gay fifth-rate vaudevillian.

A queer crowd, the fifth-rate vaudevillians. They are the outcasts. Nobody wants them. They live in a settlement of their own, whose boundaries are seldom crossed by those from the sphere of respectability. They are unconsidered. They appear; they pass; unmourned, unhonoured and unremembered. The great actor of the "legitimate" is knighted; the musical comedy star is fêted and received everywhere by the Best People; even the red-nose star of the halls is well seen. But the unsuccessful amusers of the public—their portion is weeping and gnashing of teeth. They are by turns gay and melancholy, with the despairing gaiety of the abandoned, the keen melancholy of the temperamental. They are the people who bring us laughter, who help us to forget. They invent and sing songs that put a girdle round the globe, that bring men cheerfully together in Singapore and Tobago and Honolulu and Trinidad, and are shouted under skies East and West and South; and their reward is neither here nor there; not applause or glory or motor cars or a hundred pounds a week. No; four pounds a week is theirs, with reduced rates on the railway and expenses double those of any workman or clerk. To the thoughtful person there is something infinitely pathetic in this; but by the mercy of God your fifth-rate vaudevillians are not thoughtful people. They live in, for, and by the moment; and, be their lives what they may, they are happy; for theirs is the profound wisdom of perpetual youth.

Gina's six months were filled either at the Blackwall house or at other independent halls, not controlled by the syndicates, to which her manager leased her. When not working—for the twenty-six weeks were to be filled as and when she was called—she spent her time in inspecting other shows and dancers, by the simple use of her professional card. From time to time she varied her turn, as dictated by her own moods and the vagaries of the management. Sometimes she would dance excerpts from *Coppelia* or *Sylvia*; sometimes Dvorak's *Humoreske* or *L'Automne Bacchanale*, or odds and ends from French and Russian music. But it was the sparkling sun-soaked melodies of the South, laughing of golden days and silver nights, white towns and green seas, that really held her; for to her music was melody, melody, melody—laughter, quick tears, the graceful surface of things; movement and festal colour. By instinctive choice she had already taken to her heart all Italian music—*Pagliacci, La Bohème, Rusticana, Manon*, and much of the humbler Neapolitan stuff that somehow finds its way to London. And what music was to her, so was life, and so she interpreted it to others.

Whenever she was billed, all Poplar crowded to see her; and there are still many who remember with high gratitude this lovely flower from their own gutters, and the little escapes from their sorrows that she found for them. They still remember how, passing them in the street, she, clear and steady as the dew at dawn, would but look upon them with roguish nonchalance, compel smiles from them and leave them feeling richer and stronger.

"That girl's got a heart," they would say. She shook them from pondering on their problems, lifted them into a rare, bold atmosphere, taught them how to laugh and how to feast; carried to their hearts little bouquets of solace smelling of April and May. She seemed to be born afresh each morning, so sharp and undimmed were her delight and wonder in life. She lit the whole of Poplar with her personality. The flashing of her number in the electric screen was the signal for handfuls of applause. Even those of her audience who had never before seen her went about their routine next day feeling better by remembering her. She splashed colour on their drabbery. She forced them to forget old fusty creeds of conduct, and awoke echoes in them of things that should not have been forgotten; fused into the thin body of their days something ripe and full and clustering; something, as they said, that gave 'em things to think about where before they had been fed up. She tempted them with the lure of the moment, and they followed and found that it was good. She opened new doors to them, showing them the old country to which today excursions are almost forbidden; the country of the dear brown earth and the naked flesh, of the wine-cup and flowers and kisses and Homeric laughter. She could have made a Calvinist laugh at sin. Young and wise and understanding, she would sprinkle upon it the dew of her kindly smile, and what had been bare and reprehensible a moment ago was then something tender and full of grace. Through her, all little lapses and waywardnesses became touched with delicacy. We live, we love, we die. A little while we sing in the sun, and then . . . we are gone. So let's be kind to one another; let's forgive everything; there's always an excuse. That was the Ginarian philosophy.

Twice every night she danced, and never once did she seem to "slack." After the applause welcoming her number, silence would fall on the house. The hall would be plunged sharply in a velvet gloom, through which the lights of the orchestra would gleam with subtle premonition. At a quick bell the band would blare the chord on, and the curtain would rush up on a dark blank stage. Then from between the folds of the back-cloth would steal a wee slip of a child in white, to stand poised like a startled faun. Three pale spotlights would swim from roof and wings, drift a moment, then pick her up, focusing her gleaming hair and alabaster arms.

With the conductor's tap the hall would be flooded with the ballet music of Delibes, and the dance would begin, and Gina would turn, for our delight, the loveliest pair of legs in Poplar. On the high vast stage, amid the crashing speed of the music, and the spattering fire of the side-drums, she would seem so fragile, so lost, so alone that one almost ached for her. But if she were alone at first, it was not so when she danced. At the first step she seemed to people the stage with little companies of dream. She gave us dance—and more than dance; no business of trick and limelight, but Infant Joy materialised, the lovelier because of its very waywardness. She was a poem. She was the child—naughty and bold and hungry for the beauty of life—and, through her, the audience would touch fingertips with all that was generously pure and happy. Many calls she would have at the end of her turn, and the people thought they were applauding her skill as a dancer. But a few of us knew better.

There may have been finer artists. There may have been more finished dancers. There may have been more beautiful children. But certainly never was there another woman or child who so touched her surroundings with herself, so held her audience as to send people away, full—they knew not how—of the intense glee of living. This little girl spoke to them in a language they knew, and thereby achieved the highest purpose of all art; she made others happy and strong. She changed their scowls to smiles; made them glad to meet one another. Strangers were known to speak to strangers under the spell of her dancing. Everything that is young and fresh and lovely and brave was in her message. She did so enjoy it all. That elfish little face, that lyrical body, and those twinkling toes made for the manager of the dirty hall a small fortune. Nightly she flung herself in delicate abandon through her dances, and her laugh thrilled and tickled you as does the best and gayest music. It was not the laughter of frivolity, for frivolity is but the corpse of joy; but that finer laughter expressing the full acceptance of life and all that it gives us of tears and laughter; hoping nothing, fearing nothing, but rejoicing, with sweet cynicism, in everything. It is the most heroic front that man can present to the gods that be, and Gina taught us what no school could teach us; she taught us how to wear this armour and, with its protection, to play the great game.

All Poplar loved her. The manager loved her, the stage hands loved her, the doorkeeper loved her, even her agent loved her—but unless you are of the profession, you will not appreciate the boundless significance of that. And the conductor . . . the young conductor worshipped her. He had been on his knees to her ever since that great first night. It was delicious agony for him to conduct for her. It was an irritation when her turn did not get the masses of applause that belonged to her; it was a still deeper irritation when the houseful of louts roared their appreciation. At nights he wept for her. Her face was a flower which he watered with his tears, and day by day she grew for him more and more lovely and to be desired. He had told her that he was a broken-hearted man, since the only woman he had loved, when he was eighteen, had deceived him. Gina thereafter named him the Scorched Butterfly, and would solace him with kisses.

"Makes me sick," he used to say to his first fiddle, "when I think that anything so—you know—kind of . . . lovely . . . as that should ever have to die. To think that all that . . . er . . . you know . . . glorious little body . . . should ever . . . er . . . stop living. Don't seem right. Seems like a blasted outrage to me. Ought to live for ever—anything as lovely as that. Gives me the fair fantods. And yet—of course—she will die, same as all the blasted clods and rotters like you and me. Before long, too, I shouldn't wonder. Got a kind of feeling that she will, somehow. Every time I look at her I think of it. Makes me damn sick with things. Wonder what it's all for—all this damn game of living?"

What Gina did to Poplar generally, she did also, in a more exact degree, to her immediate circle. She took Acacia Grove in hand and woke it up. She taught it how to release the flesh from its bondage and revel in the bliss of mere living. There were suppers—or rather Suppers—with the boys from one or other of the halls as guests, and cheap wine instead of beer, and sometimes a sinister little bottle of liqueur; and kisses and caresses were no longer venial sins, but little delicacies that went round the tables at these festivals as naturally as the cruet. And because Gina smiled and extolled it, they approved; and how they hastened to condemn and abolish all that upon which she frowned! She first started on Mumdear, and brought her away from the seventies and eighties into these times.

"Now, Mumdear, pull yourself together, and listen to your little Gina. In some places the younger generation knocks at the door, but in this house it's going to knock the bally door down and walk right in. You're outmoded. You've got to sit up and take notice of things more, especially of me. Don't be a back number. Come forward to the front of the bookstall. Burn that bonnet. Sell those clothes. In a word, pull yourself together. If you don't, I shall kill you, and pin you to a cork, wings extended."

And when Mumdear protested that really Gina was too young to talk like that, Gina took no notice.

"Fourteen is as fourteen does, Mumdear; and what I don't know about things a girl ought to know has been torn out of the book. I've been through things with a small-tooth comb, and I know what's there. I know the words and the music. I've read the book and seen the pictures. I've got perfect control of the ball. Brace up, old darling, and watch your Gina. It's a wise mother who knows more than her own daughter."

Thereafter there were no more newspapers for tablecloths; no more scramble suppers; no more slovenliness; no more cheap and nasty food; no more stodgy teas. The art of the Bertello home at that time was represented by oleographs after originals of Marcus Stone and the Hon. John Collier. Gina burnt them, and hung up cheap but serviceable reproductions of Whistler, Manet and Renoir. She taught Mumdear to be truly Bohemian and to entertain the boys from the profession. Mumdear blossomed anew. One final protest she ventured.

"But, Gina, duckie, we can't afford to be ikey."

"Ikey?" snapped Gina. "Who's going to be ikey, my lamb? It isn't a question of affording or of being ikey. It's a question of being comfortable. It won't cost any more to have flowers on the table and to eat something besides beef and mutton—probably less. And as for being ikey—well, when you catch me going up in the air I'll be much obliged if you'll stick pins in me so's I can explode."

As she ruled Mumdear, so did she rule others. At fourteen she had the mature carriage of womanhood—a very valuable asset in her profession. She could hold her own everywhere in the matter of back-chat, and there were none who attempted liberties a second time. It is doubtful if she had ever, at any age, had a period of innocence, using the word in the sense of ignorance. She had that curious genius for life by which the chosen divine its mysteries immediately where others perforce wait on long years of experience. As she herself expressed it, she knew her way about all the streets and wasn't going to be driven down the wrong one by any son of a gun. She might not be clever, but she thanked God she was clean.

Thus for twelve months she scattered laughter and love and kindness around Poplar, Shadwell, Limehouse and Black wall, carolling along her amiable way, joy as her counsellor, courage as her guide. Her curl-clad face at this time carried the marks of the fatigue peculiar to those temperamental subjects who spend themselves to the last ounce in whatever they set their hearts to—be it amusement, or love, or work. They live at top pitch because nothing else is possible to them. Gina's face, drawn though it was, and permanently flushed, danced always with elfin lights, and never were her limbs in repose. Even in sleep she was strangely alive, with the hectic, self-consuming energy of the precocious.

Then, as suddenly as she appeared, she disappeared, and over everything there fell a blank dismay. The light died from tne streets. Laughter was chilled. The joy of living withered as at a curse. Something tender and gay and passionate had been with us; something strange and exquisitely sweet was gone from us; and we grew sharply old and went about our work without any song or jest or caress. Only we thanked God and the grey skies that it had been given to us to recognise it while it was there.

There was some speculation, and at last, because she was so much a part of Poplar and we of her, the truth was made known sorrowfully and reverently.

A hurried night journey in a cab to a lying-in hospital; and this lovely child, fifteen years old, crept back to the bluebell or the daffodil which had lent her to us. All that remains to us is her memory and that brave philosophy of hers which was sobbed out to a few friends from the little white bed in the maternity home.

"Life's very beautiful. It's worth having, however it ends. There's so much in it. Wine and things to eat. Things to wear. Shops to look at. Coming home to supper. Meeting people. Giving parties. Books to read. Music to hear.

"I think we ought to be so happy. And so kind. Because people suffer such a lot, don't they?

"I've not been bad, Mumdear. I'm only in love with everything and everybody. They're all so . . . oh, sweet—and all that. I'm not bad. I've only loved life, and when things tempted me I said Yes. It's so easy to say No to temptation. Any coward can do that. Kiss me a little, Mum. I'm so tired.

"I hope I haven't been mean or greedy or cruel. I love the boys and girls I work with, and I love the music I dance to, and . . . Poplar.

"I don't know whether I've kept the Ten Commandments. Don't much care. But if ever I've hurt anyone, if ever I've been unkind, I hope they'll forgive me. Because . . . I . . . love them so. . . .

"Mumdear . . . ask them for some more of that cocaine . . . cos . . . it . . . it hurts . . . so."

There is a grave in East Ham cemetery which the suns and showers seem to love, so softly they fall about it. The young musical director who had presaged her ending and expressed himself as feeling sick that so fragrant a flower should ever come to die, leaves bunches of violets there once a week. For it was he who brought her to the dust.

KNIGHT-ERRANT

YOU may know Henry Wiggin on sight: Henry, the sloppily robed, the slippery faced, with hands deep in pockets, shuffling along the Limehouse streets, hugging the walls in modest self-effacement, one eye sweeping the scene before him, the other creeping sinuously to the rear; Henry, the copper's nark, the simple, the unsuspecting, knowing not the ways of deceit or the speech of the unrighteous. But Henry has of late become outmoded. After fifteen years of narking he finds that he is getting stale; he is a back number. A new generation has arisen, and with it a new school of nark diplomacy with principles very complex. Business has fallen off, the slops no longer trust him; and the exhilarating pastime of narking has become, for Henry, a weariness of the flesh. Time back, his hands, as a nark, were clean; but in these troublous days he must perforce touch jobs which, in his senescent youth, would have revolted his quick sense of nark honour.

His downfall began with that utter abandonment of principle in the Poppy Gardens excitement. And, if you possess a sufficiently adventurous spirit to penetrate into those strange streets where the prudent never so much as peep, and to hazard inquiries concerning Henry the Blahsted Nark, the full explanation, which follows below, will be given you—though in an amplified form, richer in the vivid adjective.

It is now known that it was no professional point that led him to slide back on the one person in the world who was more to him than gold or silver or many beers. It was something more tremendous, more incomprehensible, more . . . you know. The two people concerned are unfortunately inaccessible to the general public and even to the ubiquitous pressman. Both of them, in their different ways, shrink from notoriety with a timidity as sharp as that which distinguishes the lady novelist. But pressmen are not the only people who can get stories. Here is Henry's.

Henry had a brother, a dearly loved companion, whom, from infancy, he had cherished with a love that is not usual among brothers under the Poplar arches. For this brother he had, when a nipper, pinched from coffee-stalls, so that he should not go supperless to bed. He had "raked" and "glimmed," and on two occasions he was caught doing honest work for his young brother. The one soft spot in his heart was for brother Bert. But this brother . . . Alas, how often does one find similar cases in families! Two brothers may be brought up amid the same daily surroundings, under the same careful parentage, enjoying each the same advantages. Yet, while one pursues the bright and peaceful path of virtue, the other will deviate to the great green ocean of iniquity. It is idle to shirk the truth. Let the sordid fact be admitted. While Henry Wiggin was a copper's nark, brother Bert was a burglar. He stole things, and sold them to Mr. Fence Cohen round the corner, and was not ashamed. Henry knew that this was wrong, and the dishonesty of his brother was a load to him. Often he had sought to lead those erring feet into the Straight Way, but his fond efforts were repulsed.

"'Enery—if yeh don't stop shootin' yeh mouth at me, I'll push yeh blasted face in!"

On the great night when Romance peeped coyly into the life of Henry Wiggin, he and Bert were noisily guzzling fried fish and taters and draught stout in their one-room cottage, back of the Poplar arches—Number 2 Poppy Gardens. Poppy Gardens, slumbrous and alluring as its name may be, is neither slumbrous nor alluring. Rather, it is full of quick perils for the unwary. It has not only its record of blood, but also its record of strange doings which can only be matched by the records of certain byways about Portman Square. The only difference is that in the one place you have dirt, decay, and yellow and black faces. In the other, you have luxury and gorgeous appurtenance.

Wherefore it was stupid, stupid, with that ostrichlike stupidity that distinguishes the descendants of noble families who have intermarried with their kind; I say it was stupid for Lady Dorothy Grandolin to choose this, of all places, for her first excursion into slumland, in order to gather material for her great work: *Why I am a Socialist: a Confession of Faith; Together with some Proposals for Ameliorating the Condition of the Very Poor; with Copious Appendices by the Fabian Society.* Far better might she have fared in the Dials; in Lambeth; even in Hoxton. But no; it must be Limehouse—and at night. Really, one feels that she deserved all she got.

With no other escort than a groom—who knew a chap down here—she stood in West India Dock Road, near the Asiatics' Home; and, to be strictly impartial, she was a rather effective bit of colour, so far as raiment went. You have certainly seen her photographs in the sixpenny weeklies, or reproductions, in *The Year's Pictures*, of those elegant studies by Sargent and Shannon. It cannot be said that she is beautiful, though the post card public raves about her; for her beauty is classical and Greek, which means that she is about as interesting as a hardboiled egg. However, if we acknowledge her divinity we must regret that she should ever have embraced the blue-serge god, and regret still more that her waxen fingers should have itched with the fever of propagandist authorship. However, she was determined to do a book on the Very Poor; nothing would stop her. Her little soul blazed in a riot of fine fire for the cause. Yesterday, it was Auction; the day before it was Settlements; today, the Very Poor. And in papa's drawing-room there was no doubt that the Very Poor was a toy to be played with very prettily; for it is the one success of these people that they can do things with an air.

So she stood in the damp darkness of Little Asia, skirts daintily aloof, while the groom sought for the chap he knew down here. She felt that it must be a queer and inspiring situation to know a man down here. Yet Dixon seemed to think nothing of it. It seemed too frightfully awful that people should live here. Never mind; Socialism was growing day by day among the right people, and——

Then Dixon returned with the chap he knew down there, and Lady Dorothy thought of Grosvenor Square, and shrank as she viewed their cicerone. For he was Ho Ling, fat and steamy; and he sidled to her out of the mist, threatening and shrinking, with that queer mixture of self-conceit and self-contempt which is the Chinese character. It may be that Dixon was up to something in bringing his mistress here; one never knows. But here she was, and here was the yellow Ho Ling; and, with a feminine fear of cowardice, she nerved herself to go through with it. She had heard that the Chinese quarter offered splendid material for studies in squalor, as well as an atmosphere of the awful and romantic. Her first glances did not encourage her in this idea; for these streets and people are only awful and romantic to those who have awful and romantic minds. Lady Dorothy hadn't. She had only awful manners.

With Ho Ling in front, Lady Dorothy following, and Dixon in the rear, they crossed the road.

*　　*　　*

Henry Wiggin lifted the jug from the coverless deal table, inverted it on his face, held it for a moment, then set it down with a crack, voluptuously rolling his lips. That was all right, that was. Heaven help the chaps what hadn't got no beer that night; that's all he'd got to say. He was leading from this to a few brief but sincere observations to his brother Bert on the prices of malt liquors, when, on the grimy window, which, in the fashion of the district, stood flush with the pavement, came two or three secret taps. Each started; each in different ways. Henry half rose from his chair, and became at once alert, commanding, standing out. Bert's glance shot to half-a-dozen points at once, and he seemed to dissolve into himself. For a few seconds the room was chokingly silent. Then, with a swift, gliding movement, Henry reached the window, and, as Bert flung back from the light's radius, he stealthily opened it. It creaked yearningly, and immediately a yellow face filled its vacancy.

"Ullo. It is I—Ho Ling. Lady here—all same lah-de-dah—going—how you say—slumming. Parted half-a-bar. Wants to see inside places. Will my serene friend go halves if she come into here, and part more half-bars? How you say?"

"Wotto. I'm on. Wait 'alf-a-jiff." He closed the window, and made for the door. "'S all right, Bert. On'y a toff gointer shell out. Wants to squint round our place. We go halves with Chinky whatever she parts."

"Sure it's a toff?" in a voice meant to be a whisper but suggesting the friction of sandpaper. "Sure it ain't a plant?"

"Course it ain't. Old 'O Ling's all right." He fiddled with the handle of the door, opened it, and stood back, only mildly interested in the lah-de-dah who was invading the privacy of his home. If he had any feeling at all, it was a slight impatience of this aloof creature of the world above; the sort of mild irritation that the convicts feel when they stand on railway stations, the objects of the curious stares of hundreds of people who are at liberty and think nothing of being so.

There was a moment's hesitation; then, into the fishy, beery, shaggy atmosphere of the room stole a whiff of the ampler ether and diviner air of Mayfair. Into the arc of yellow candlelight, into the astonished gaze of Henry, and into the professionally quickened stare of Bert, stepped the warm, human actuality of *A Duke's Daughter*, from last year's academy. Behind her, in the doorway, calm and inscrutable as a Pentonville warder, stood Ho Ling, careful to be a witness of the amount parted. Behind him, in the deep, dark gloom of the archway, was the groom.

Lady Dorothy gazed around. She saw a carpetless room, furnished only with a bed on the floor, a couple of chairs, and a table littered with fried fish and chips and a couple of stone jugs. In the elusive twilight, it was impossible to obtain a single full view, and the bobbing candle made this still more difficult. By the table stood Henry, in all his greasy glory, a tasteful set-off to the walls which dripped with moisture from the railway above.

Oh! And again—oh! And did people really live down here? Was it allowed? Didn't the authorities——? Was this all there was—one room? Did they eat and sleep and do *everything* here? And was this all the furniture? Really? But *however* did they manage? Did they really mean to say . . . But they couldn't, surely . . . How . . . well . . . Was that the bed—that thing over there? And had they no . . . Dear, dear. How terrible. How——

Oh! What was that? A rat? A *rat*? Ugh! How *horrid!* She skipped lightly aside, and as she did so the bracelets on her wrists jingled, and the small chatelaine bag at her waist jingled, and her wristwatch and the brooch at her alabaster throat were whipped to a thousand sparkling fragments by the thin light. And as they sang, Bert's ears tingled, even as a warhorse's at the noise of battle.

He considered the situation. From the outer world came little sound. The bewildering maze of arches shut them completely from the rattle of the main streets, and Poppy Gardens was deserted. A train rumbled heavily over the arches—a long train carrying a host of woes that grumbled and whined. It passed, and left a stillness more utter. It was simply tempting Providence to let the occasion pass. It was simply asking for it.

He looked; he saw; he appreciated. His fingers moved. On her entry he had been standing back in the corner, beyond the dancing reach of the light, and, with subconscious discretion, he had maintained his position. Now he saw the magnificent meaning of it. And as Lady Dorothy, prettily shrinking, moved from point to point of the cramped room, he thrust forward his scrubby lips until they reached Henry's shoulder.

"It's a sorf job!"

Henry at the table turned his head, and his eyes raked the ceiling. "I'm ashamed of yeh, Bert," he whispered.

"Make old Ling take that kid off," came from Bert. "Tell 'im we'll share."

"Bert—oh, yeh low blaggard!"

But Bert, from his gloomy corner, caught Ho Ling's eye, and mouthed him. And Ho Ling knew. He turned back into the dark street. He spoke to the groom, and his mumbling voice came sleepily to the others, like the lazy hum of busy bees. Four footsteps grated on the rough asphalt and gradually dimmed away. Silence.

Bert moved a foot forward, and tapped his brother's ankle. There was no response. He repeated the action. But Henry had dropped into his chair before the odorous litter of three-pieces-and-chips in paper, and was staring, staring, quietly but with passionate adoration, at the lady who shed her lambent light on Number 2 Poppy Gardens. For though Henry's calling, if it is to be followed with success—and five years ago Henry was the narkiest nark in East London—demands a hardened cynicism, a resolute stoniness, yet his heart was still young, in places, and a faint spark of humanity still glowed, not only for Bert, but for the world in general. But Henry knew nothing of the ways of love. None of the rosebuds of Limehouse had won his regard or even his fleeting fancy. In his middle age he was heartwhole. And now, into the serenity of that middle age had burst a whirlwind. He gazed—and gazed. Here stood this—this—"ayngel" was the only word that came to his halting mind—here she stood, a rose among dank river weeds, in his bedroom, next to him, 'Enery, the blahsted copper's nark. It was too wonderful. It was too—oh, too . . .

He was trapped. He was in love. Soft voices sang to him, and he became oblivious to all save the dark head of Dorothy, standing out in the misty light, a vague circle of radiance enchanting his dulled eyes.

So that Bert tapped his brother's foot vainly.

Then Dorothy moved a pace toward Henry. Bert, still unseen, drew snakily back. She stood against the table, looking down on the seated figure. Her dress rustled against his fingers, and he thrilled with pulsing heat, because of the body loaded with graces and undiscovered wonders that it clothed. The glamour of her close neighbourhood and the peaceful perfume of violet that stole from her fired him with a senseless glory, and he longed to assert his right to her admiration. She was talking, but he heard no words. He only knew that she was standing against him; and as he stared, unseeing, about the room with its whiffy table, its towzled bed, its scratched walls (set alight by the shivering candle, as though the whole world were joining him in his tremor), he felt well content. He would like to sit like this for ever and for ever. This English rose, this sleek angel, this . . .

Ah! Henry felt at that moment that it was Providence and nothing less. Providence. Only so could it be explained. It was, without the least doubt, some divinity protecting this wandering angel that moved Henry, at that critical moment, to turn his head. For what he saw, as he turned, was a corner of thick velvety darkness; and from that corner emerged a pair of swart, whiskered hands. Slowly they swam, slowly, toward the fair neck of Lady Dorothy as she talked to Henry in ostrichlike security. Henry stared.

Then the hands met, and their meeting was signalled by a quick scream that died as soon as uttered into a gasping flutter. It must be repeated that Henry loved his brother, and though, from childhood onward, they had differed widely on points of ethics, never once had either raised his hand against the other. But tonight romance had steeped Henry's soul; he was moon-mad; the fairies had kissed him. Thus he explained it next morning, but none would hear him.

For, the moment Bert's hands enclosed Dorothy's neck, Henry, full of that tough, bony strength peculiar to those who live lives of enforced abstinence, sprang up, and his left went *thk!* squarely between Bert's eyes. The grasp was loosened, and Henry grabbed Dorothy's wrist and swung back his arm, jerking her clean across the room. She screamed. He followed it with a second blow on Bert's nose. Bert staggered, dazed.

"Wha'—wha'? Hands orf yeh brother, 'Enery. What yeh doin'? 'Ittin' yer own brother?" There was ineffable surprise and reproach in his tone.

But Henry left him in no doubt, for he now saw red, and a third smack landed on Bert's jaw. Then Bert, too, arose in his wrath. Henry, however, in his professional career had had vast experience in tough scrums of this kind, in narrow space, while Bert knew but little of any warfare except that of the streets. As Henry drew back, tightly strung for Bert's rush, his leg shot out behind him, caught the corner of the table and sent it and the candle sprawling to the floor with a doleful bump and a rush of chips.

Then the fun began. For of all sports that can ever be devised, there can be none more inspiriting than a fight in the dark. To Henry, in the peculiar circumstances, it was the time of his life. He thrilled and burned with the desire to perform great deeds. He would have liked very much to die in this fight. Quixote never so thrilled for Dulcinea as Henry Wiggin for Lady Dorothy. He became all-powerful; nothing was impossible. He could have fought a thousand Berts and have joyed in the encounter. An intense primed vigour swept over his spare jockey frame, and he knew, even so late, the meaning of life and love. Lady Dorothy screamed.

"Oh, yeh snipe!" cried Bert, with furious curses; and his rubber slippers *sup-supped* on the floor as he fumbled for his recreant brother. Henry retreated to the wall, and his pawing hand found Lady Dorothy. She screamed and shrank.

"Shut up, yeh fool!" he cried, in excess of enthusiasm. "Give yehself away, yeh chump. Steady—I'll get yeh out." He dragged her along the wall while Bert fumed and panted like a caged animal.

"Gotcher!" A sudden rush forward and he spread himself over the upturned table. More language, and Lady Dorothy, had her senses been fully alert, might have culled material for half-a-dozen slum novels from her first excursion into Limehouse.

"'Alf a mo', 'alf a mo'," whispered Henry, consolingly, as he felt her shake against him. "I'll get the door in a minute. So bloody dark, though. Steady—'e's close now. Bert—don' be a fool. Yeh'll get the rozzers on yeh."

But Bert was beating the air with a Poplar sandbag, and it was clear from his remarks that he was very cross. It seemed doubtful that he would hear reason. Lady Dorothy screamed.

"'Alf a mo', lidy. I'll——" He broke off with a rude word, for the sandbag had made its mark on his shoulder. Now he wanted Bert's blood as a personal satisfaction, and he left his lady by the wall and charged gloriously into the darkness. "I'll break yeh face if I get yeh, Bert. I'll split yeh lousy throat."

His hand groped and clawed; it touched something soft. The something darted back, and almost immediately came a volley of throttled screams that set Henry writhing with a lust for blood. There followed a little clitter, as of dropping peas, and a wrench and a snap.

"Gottem!"

"Bert—yeh bleeding twicer, if I get 'old of yeh I'll——" and the rest of his speech cannot be set down. He snaked along the wall and his stretched hand struck the door knob. The situation was critical. The thick darkness veiled everything from him. Somewhere, in that pool of mystery, was Lady Dorothy in the vandal clutches of brother Bert. Too, she was silent. Henry opened the door, and looked out on a darkness and a silence thicker than those of the room. A train rumbled over the long-suffering arches. When it had faded into the beyond, he stepped out and put one hand to his mouth. Along the hollow, draughty archway a queer call rang in a little hurricane.

"Weeny—Weeny—*Wee-ee-ee-ee-ny!*"

Bert gave a gusty scream. He knew what it meant. "Gawd, 'Enery, I'll do yeh in for this, I'll 'ave——"

"Where'bouts are yeh, lidy; whereabouts are yeh?"

"I'm here. He's got—he's—oh!" Tiny shrieks flitted from her like sparks from an engine.

And then the atmosphere became electric, as Henry, noting the position of the door, made a second dash into space. He heard the dragging of feet as Bert hustled his quarry away from the point at which she had spoken. He followed it, and this time he caught Bert and held him. For a moment or so they strained terribly; then Henry, with a lucky jerk, released the grip on Dorothy.

They closed. Henry got a favourite armlock on his brother, but blood was pounding and frothing, and violence was here more useful than skill. They stood rigid, and gasped and swore as terribly as our Army in Flanders, and they tugged and strained with no outward sign of movement. One could hear the small bones crick. Lady Dorothy stood in a corner and shrieked staccato. It seemed that neither would move for the next hour, when Bert, seeing a chance, shifted a foot for a closer grip, and with that movement the fight went to Henry. He gave a sudden jerk and twist, flattened his brother against his hard chest, hugged him in a bearlike embrace for a few seconds and swung him almost gently to the ground.

"Come, lidy—quick. 'E'll be up in a minute. Run! Fer the love of glory—run!"

He caught her and slid for the door; bumped against the corner of it; swore; found the exit and pulled Lady Dorothy, gasping thankfully, into the chill air and along the sounding arches, which already echoed the throbbing of feet—big feet. But he had no thought for what lay behind. With Dorothy's lily hand clasped in his he raced through the night and the lone Poplar arches towards East India Dock Road.

* * *

"No, but, look 'ere," said Bert; "hang it all, cancher see——"

"Quite 'nough from you," said the constable. "Hear all that at the station, we can."

Bert extended a hand tragically to argue, but, realising the futility of resisting the obvious, he sat on the edge of the floor-bed and relapsed into moody silence. He reflected on the utter hopelessness of human endeavour while such a thing as luck existed. And it was only the other day that he had pasted on his walls a motto, urging him to *Do It Now*. "You was 'asty, Bert," he communed. "'At's alwis bin your fault—'aste."

Then Henry, shoulders warped, hands pocketed, shuffled into the room. He looked disgustedly at the floor, littered with fish and chips and watered with two small pools of black beer. He looked around the room, as though around life generally, and his lip dropped and his teeth set. He seemed to see nobody.

"What-o, Hen, me boy!" said the constable amiably. "You look cheerful, you do. Look's though you lost a tanner and found a last year's Derby sweep ticket."

Then, relapsing to business: "This is all right, though, this is." He indicated the table, where lay a little heap of bracelets, a brooch, two or three sovereigns, some silver and a bag. "First time I ever knew you pop the daisy on yer brother, though. Fac. What was it?"

"Eh? What was . . . ? Oh, he went for a—a lidy what was going round 'ere. She's just got int'er carriage near 'The Star of the East.' You'll find 'er chap under the arches somewhere with old Ho Ling, the Chink. In 'The Green Man' I fink I saw 'em. Bert went for 'er and swabbed the twinklers.

'At's all I know." He sat down sourly by the table.

Bert sprang up frantically, but the constable put a spry grip on his arm. He squirmed. "What . . . No, but . . . What yeh doing . . . 'ere . . . I . . . Narkin' on yer own brother! But yeh can't! Yeh can't *do* it! Playin' the low-down nark on Bert. You . . . I . . ."

It could be seen that this second shock was too terrible. The fight and the calling of the cops was a mortal offence, but at least understandable. But this . . .

"'Ere, but it's Bert, 'Enery. Bert. You ain't goin' back on ol' Bert. Now! 'Enery, play up!" He implored with hands and face.

Henry slewed savagely round. In his eyes was the light that never was on sea or land. "Oh, shut orf!"

For the lips of Henry Wiggin, copper's nark, had kissed those of Lady Dorothy Grandolin, all under the Poplar arches, and in the waistcoat pocket of Henry Wiggin, the copper's nark, were the watch and chain of Lady Dorothy Grandolin.

THE GORILLA AND THE GIRL

IN an underground chamber near the furtive Causeway, Saturnalia was being celebrated. The room which lay below the sign of the Blue Lantern was lit by shy gas-jets and furnished with wooden tables and chairs. Strange scents held the air. Bottled beer and whisky crowded a small table at the far end, and near this table stood the owner of the house, Mr. Hunk Bottles. At other small tables were cards and various devices for killing time and money. All those who were well seen in Limehouse and Poplar were here, and the informed observer could recognise many memorable faces. Chuck Lightfoot and Battling Burrows were engaged in a comparatively peaceable game of fan-tan with Sway Lim and Quong Tart; at any rate the noise they were making could not have been heard beyond Custom House. Tai Ling and his Marigold were there, very merry, and Pansy Greers, with an escort from the Pool, attracted much attention in a dress which finished where it ought to have begun. Ding-Dong was there: Perce Sleep; Paris Pete; Polly the Pug; Jenny Jackson's Provence Boys, so called because they frequented that café; the Chatwood Kid, from whom no safe could withhold its secrets; and, in fact, all the golden boys and naughty girls of the district were snatching their moment of solace. Old Foo Ah lolloped on a chair, slumbering in the heavy content of a kangaroo. That masculine lady, Tidal Basin Sal, sprawled on a shabby private-bar lounge with a little girl, whom she would alternately kiss and slap proprietorially. A man from the Polynesians made himself a nuisance to the air and the company; and on a table at the extreme end stood little Gina of the Chinatown, slightly drunk, and with clothing disarranged, singing that most thrilling and provocative of ragtimes:

"You're here and I'm here,
So what do we care?"

"Yerss," the Monico Kid was saying, in a sedulously acquired American accent, "had a tumble today. I was hustling the match with Flash Fred, and we took a big nig off the water for the works. I stood for the finish on him, and it listens like good music to me, cos he don't tip me. Fred spotted him and officed me to pull the rough stuff. Rough's my middle name. I wrote the book about it. But the nig was fresh and shouted for the blue boys. See my eye? Well, we handed out some punk stuff, and then I levanted, and now I'm lying cavey a bit, see? Gaw, there ain't nothing to this roughneck stuff. I figger on quittin' 'fore long. Dick the Duke was pinched t'other day. I went t'ear it. A stretch? Lorlummy, they fair shied the book at 'im and told 'im to add up the sentences. Yerss . . . it's all a wangle."

But the couple on whom Hunk kept the most careful eye were his young daughter, Lois, and little Batty Bertello, the son of the sharpest copper's nark in the quarter. These two sat apart, on a lounge, clasped in one another's arms, their feet drawn up from the floor, lip locked to lip in the ecstasy of self-discovery; for the man the ecstasy of possession, for the girl the ecstasy of surrender.

Lois had picked up Batty in Tunnel Gardens one Sunday night, and although from the age of ten she had been accustomed to kisses and embraces from boy admirers, she realised, when Batty first kissed her, that here was something different. There was nothing soppy about him . . . rather, something kind of curious . . . big and strong, like. He seemed to give everything; yet gave you the rummy feeling of having held something in reserve, something that you were not good enough for. You didn't know what it was or how great it was, and it made you kind of mad to find out. And when he kissed you . . . She wondered if she were a bad, nasty girl for wanting to have his hands about her. All her person was at once soothed and titillated by the throb of his pulses when they clasped; she was a responsive instrument on which he played the eternal melody. She felt that she could hold no secrets from him; so at risk of losing him she told him the whole truth about herself; told it in that voice of hers, fragile and firm as fluted china and ringing with the tender tones of far-away bells. How that she was the daughter of the terrible Hunk Bottles, and lived in that bad house, the Blue Lantern, and how that her father was the lifelong enemy of his father, Jumbo Bertello. And Batty had laughed, and they had continued to love.

Presently Lois swung herself from the lounge and began to "cook" for her boy. On a small table she spread the layout; lit the lamp; dug out the treacly hop from the toey and held it against the flame. It bubbled furiously, and the air was charged with a loathsome sweetness. Then, holding the bamboo pipe in one hand, she scraped the bowl with a yen-shi-gow, and kneaded the brown clot with the yen-hok. Slowly it changed colour as the poison gases escaped. Then she broke a piece in her finger, and dropped it into the bowl, and handed the stem to Batty. He puffed languorously, and thick blue smoke rolled from him.

But Hunk Bottles regarded the scene with slow anger. Lois was ignoring his commands. When he had heard that she was going with the son of a copper's nark he had drawn her aside and had spoken forceful words. He had said:

"Look 'ere, me gel, you be careful. Less you go round with that young Bertello the better. Y'know what 'is old man is, doncher? Well, be careful what yeh talk about. Cos if any of my business gets out . . . Well" (he hit the air with a fat hand) "if I do catch yeh talkin' at all, I'll break every bone in yeh blinkin' body. I'll take the copper-stick to yeh and won't let up till every bit of yeh's broken. Else I'll give yeh to one o' the Chinks to do what 'e likes with. So now yeh know. See?"

Lois knew that this was not an idle threat. She had seen things done at the Blue Lantern. There were rooms into which she was not permitted to pry. Once in the cellar she had seen little glass tubes of peculiar shape, coloured papers, and a big machine. She had seen men who came to the private bar, and never called for a drink, but had one given them, and who sat and mumbled across the counter for hours at a stretch.

And Batty . . . he, too, knew a bit. He wanted to take her away from the lowering Causeway and the malefic air of the quarter. But he knew that old Hunk would never consent to marriage; Lois was too useful in the bar as a draw to custom. He knew, too, that if he took her forcibly away Hunk would be after them and would drag her back. The only way by which he could get her would be to remove Hunk for a spell, and the only means by which this could be accomplished. . . . At this point he saw clear. Very little stood between Hunk and the Thames Police Court. A little definite evidence and old Jumbo Bertello could work a raid at the right moment.

So, the night after the Saturnalia, he took Lois for a bus-ride, and he talked and talked to her. She told him what her dad would do to her if . . . But he dashed in and assured her that there was not one moment's danger to her little dear body; not a moment's. One tiny scrap of evidence in his hands and she would be safe with him for ever.

Well, that night certain pieces of coloured paper passed from the hands of Lois to those of her Batty, and from Batty they passed to the old copper's nark. Jumbo hugged those pieces of coloured paper in his breast-pocket and was glad. He would go straight to the station and deposit them, and thus he would be helping his kid to marry the girl he wanted and would also be helping himself to rewards of a more substantial kind. He passed the Star of the East, and noted mechanically that it was closing time; but he noted with a very actual interest that a crowd had assembled at a near corner. Now Jumbo was a man of simple tastes. Above all else he loved the divine simplicity of a fight, and a street crowd acted on him as a red rag on a bull. At such a spectacle his eyes would light up, his nostrils quiver, his hands clench and unclench and his feet dance a double shuffle until, unable longer to remain neutral, he would charge in and lend a hand to whichever party in the contest seemed to be getting the worse. So it was tonight. Within half-a-minute he was in the centre of the crowd. At the end of the full minute he was prostrate on the ground, his skull cracked on the edge of the kerb.

* * *

The inquest was held on the following day, and the full report in the local paper contained the following passage:—

"The deceased was known in the district as a man who has, on frequent occasions, been of material assistance to the police in the carrying out of their duties in the Dockside. In his pockets were found 1s. 6½d. in coppers and several slips of crisp, coloured paper of a curious quality unknown to any of the papermakers in London. It is understood that the police are pursuing inquiries."

Old Hunk Bottles came down to supper in the parlour of the Blue Lantern at half-past eight that evening, and while Lois ministered to him with parched face and a trembling hand he called for the local paper. The skin of her whole body seemed to go white and damp, and her sunset hair took fire. She saw him turn to the police-court reports and inquests. She saw him read, with a preliminary chuckle of satisfaction, the report on the death of the copper's nark. And then, like a rabbit before a snake, she shrank against the wall as she saw his face change, and the paper droop from his hands. Very terrible were the eyes that glared at her. She would have made a rush for the door, but every nerve of her was sucked dry. Then the glare faded from his face and he became curiously natural.

"Well," he remarked, "bits of coloured paper don't prove much, do they? Let 'em make all the inquiries they like about their bits of coloured paper. They won't git far on that. But there's one thing that bits of coloured paper do prove when they're in old Jumbo's pockets, and that is, that you're going through it tonight, me gel. Right through it."

She cuddled the wall and hunched her shoulders as though against an immediate blow.

"Ar, you can skulk, yeh little copper's nark, but yer in for it now. What d'I tell yeh? Eh?" He spoke in syrupy tones, terribly menacing. "What d'I tell yeh I'd do? Answer, yeh skunk, answer! Come on!" He approached her with a quick step and snatched her wrists from her face. "Answer me.

What d'I say I'd do to yeh?"

"Break every bone in me body," she whimpered.

"That's right. But I changed me mind. It'll make too much noise round the Blue Lantern. I got something better for you, me darling. Y'know our top room?"

She was silent, and he shook her like a dog. "Answer! Know our top room?"

"Yes, dad."

"Where we keep old Kang Foo's gorilla what he brought from the Straits?"

"Yes, dad."

"Well, the safest place for little copper's narks is a top room where they can't get out. That's where you're going tonight. Going to be locked in the top room with old Kang's gorilla. 'E'll look after yeh all right. That'll learn yeh to keep yeh tongue quiet. See? That's what I'm going to do. Lock you in the dark room with the big monkey. And if yeh don't know what a gorilla can do to a gel when it gets 'er alone, yeh soon will. So now!"

"Oh . . . dad. . . ." She blubbered, a sick dread filling all her face. "I di'n' do nothing. I dunno nothin' 'bout it," she lied. "I dunno nothing. I ain't been blabbin'."

"Aw, yeh damn little liar!" He lifted a large hand over her. "I'll give yeh somethin' extra for lyin' if yeh don't cut it. Now then, up yeh go and sleep with little 'Rilla. No nonsense."

What happened then was not pleasant to see. She struggled. She screamed hoarse screams which made scarce any sound. She kicked and bit. Her dramatic hair tumbled in a torrent. And her big father flung two arms about her, mishandled her, and dragged her with rattling cries up the steep stair. When they reached the top landing, to which she had never before ascended, and the loft of a room which, she had heard, Kang Foo rented as a stable for his gorilla, all fight was gone from her. A limp, moaning bundle was flung into the thickly dark room. She heard the rattle of a chain as though the beast had been unloosed, and then the door slammed and clicked, and she was alone with the huge, hairy horror.

In a sudden access of despairing strength she rushed to the window, barred inside and out, and hammered with soft fists and screamed: "Help! Help! Dad's locked me up with a monkey!"

It was about half-an-hour later that one came to Batty Bertello, who was taking a glass to the memory of the deceased dad and also to buck himself up a bit, and told him that he had passed the Blue Lantern and had heard a girl's voice screaming from a top window something about being shut up with a monkey. And Batty, who suddenly realised that Hunk Bottles had heard of those slips of paper, dropped his glass and, with love-madness in his face, dashed for the door, crying:

"Come on, boys! All of yeh! Old Hunk's murdering his Lois!"

And the boys, scenting a fight, went on. They didn't know where the fight was or whom they were going to fight. It was sufficient that there was a fight. Through brusque streets and timid passages they chased Batty, and when he broke, like a crash of thunder, into the private bar, they followed him.

"Over, boys!" he cried, and to the intense delight of all he placed a hand on the bar and vaulted the beer engines, bringing down only two glasses. Fired by his example, they followed, and then Hunk Bottles was rushed to the ropes by the crowd—that is, to the farther wall of his own parlour. They lowered upon him; they beetled, arms ready for battle. In the front centre was the alert Batty.

"Where's Lois?"

"G-gone to bed!" answered Hunk, taken aback by the sudden invasion. Then, attempting to recover: "'Ere, what the devil's all this? 'Ere—Joe, fetch the cops. 'Ere—I——"

"Shut up!" snapped Batty. "Liar. You shut 'er up with a monkey upstairs."

"Liar, I 'aven't!"

"Liar, you 'ave!"

"Yerss, you 'ave!" roared the crowd, not knowing what it was he had done. "Down 'im, boys. Dot 'im one. Cop 'old o' Joe—don't let 'im out."

The potman was dragged also into the parlour and the few loungers in the four-ale bar took the opportunity to come round and help themselves to further drinks. "'E's shut Lois up with a monkey. Aw—dirty dog. Less go up and get 'er out."

But then the potman cried upon them: "Don' be damn fools. Wod yer talkin' about. 'Ow *can* 'e shut 'er up wiv a monkey—eh? Yer plurry pie-cans! 'Ow can 'e? We ain't got no monkey 'ere!"

"Liar!" cried everybody, as a matter of principle.

"I ain't a liar. Go an' see fer yehselves. We ain't got no monkey 'ere. Ain't 'ad one 'ere for nearly a year. Old Kang Foo sold his to Bostock. Don' make such damn fools o' yesselves. Nothin' ain't been done to the gel. Old 'Unk's on'y punished 'er cos she's too chippy. She's 'is daughter. Got a right to, ain't 'e? If she'd bin mine I'd 'ave give 'er a good spankin'. 'E's on'y sent 'er up to the room to frighten 'er. It's empty—absolutely empty."

"Then what's the screamin' and rowin' that's bin going on all the time? Eh? Listen!"

Low noises came from above. "Cos she's frightened—'at's why. There's nothin' there."

"Yerss, that's it," said the aggrieved Hunk, still wedged against the wall by the crowd. "Yeh makin' yesselves dam fools. Specially this dam little snipe, son of a copper's nark. Go up and see fer yesselves since yeh so pushin'. Go on—up yeh go. She's all right—quiet enough now, cos she's found out there's nothing there. I on'y sent 'er there to get a fright. There warn't no blasted monkey there."

"Well, we know the kind o' swine you are, Hunk. Don't stand arguin' there. Get on up!"

"I ain't a-arguin' wiv yer. I'm a-telling of yeh. We ain't got no monkey. Not fer a year. So now. Go on up and see fer yesselves, yeh dirty lot of poke-noses. She ain't 'urt; on'y scared. Half-a-hour in a dark room'll learn 'er to be'ave, and it wouldn't do some of you no 'arm. Go on! Get up my clean stairs and knock everything to pieces, yeh pack of flat-faced pleading chameleons!" He stopped and spluttered and shook himself with impotent anger. Any one of the crowd he could have put on the floor with one hand, but he recognised that a gang was a gang, and he accepted the situation. He flung a hand to the stair. "Go on—up yeh go—the 'ole pleadin' lot of yeh!"

So up they went.

At the top of the house all was very still. The sounds of the river came in little low laps. The noises of the street were scarcely heard at all. They paused in a body at the door. The potman was with them with the key. He unlocked the door, shoved it with a casual hand, and piped:

"Come on, kid—come on out. Some of yeh lovely narky friends think we bin murderin' yeh." The boys clustered in an awkward bunch at the door, peering into the darkness. But nobody came out; nobody answered; no sound at all was to be heard. "Strike a light!" shouted a voice. Far below, the silence was bespattered with muddy laughter from the four-ale bar.

The light was brought, and they crowded in. On the bare floor of the room lay Lois. Portions of her clothing were strewn here and there. Her released hair rippled mischievously over her bosom disclosed to the waist. Her stiff hands were curled into her disordered dress. She was dead. The room was otherwise empty.

DING-DONG-DELL

TOM THE TINKER came off the lighter in mid-stream near Limehouse Hole, and was taken to the landing-stage in an absurdly small rowboat. His face was cold and grey, his clothes damp and disordered. He had been on a job. Under the uncommunicative Limehouse night the river ran like a stream of molten lead. Stately cargoes pranced here and there. Fussy little tugs champed upstream. Sirens wailed their unhappy song. Slothful barges rolled and drifted, seeming without home or haven. Cranes creaked and blocks rattled, and far-away Eastern voices were usually expressive in chanties. But Tom the Tinker saw and heard nothing of this. He had not that queer faculty, indispensable to the really successful cracksman, of paying rapt attention to six things at once. He could only concentrate on one thing at a time, and, while that faculty may serve in commerce and office business, it will not serve in the finer, larger spheres of activity. Here are wanted the swift veins, the clear touch, imagination in directed play; every tissue straining at the leash, ready to be off in whatsoever direction the quarry may turn.

Tom the Tinker, I say, saw only one thing at a time, and on this occasion he was concerned with the nice arrangement of the Bethnal Green jewellery rampage. He did not, therefore, on arriving home, observe the distracted manner of his wife.

When he entered the kitchen of his house in Pekin Street, Poplar, he noted that she was there; and that was all. The merest babe, though preoccupied with burglary preparations, would have noted more. He kissed her, perfunctorily. She wound both arms about him, also perfunctorily.

"Ding-Dong been here?" he asked.

She said: "Yes, Ding-Dong's been."

"Anything to say?"

"Nope," she replied, and continued to puff her cigarette.

He sat down, lifted a smoke from her store, and lit it. His eyes fell to the floor; his hands sought his pockets. His wife looked swiftly at him. He might have been asleep.

She was a woman who had passed the flush of girlhood, but was not yet old; twenty-nine, maybe; old enough in those parts, though. Still, there were some who had looked upon her and found her not altogether to be despised. There was, for example, Ding-Dong. Somehow, her mouth always tightened when she thought of Ding-Dong; tightened, not in vexation or as a mouth tightens when about to speak hard words, but as a mouth tightens when about to receive and return a kiss. As she sat staring upon her lawful mate, Tom the Tinker, she recalled a certain amiable night when Tom had been giving his undivided ttention to a small job—he only worked the small jobs—in Commercial Road, which had long needed his services.

Do you remember that little four-ale bar, the Blue Lantern, in Limehouse, and the times we used to have there with that dear drunken devil, Jumbo Brentano? Well, it was there, amid the spiced atmosphere of the Orient and under that pallid speck of blue flame, that Jumbo Brentano introduced Ding-Dong to Tom the Tinker as a likely apprentice. His recommendation had taken the form that young Ding-Dong was one of the blasted best; that he'd give his last penny away to a pal; that he'd got the pluck of the devil, where danger was concerned; the guts of a man, where enterprise was concerned; and the heart of a woman, where fidelity and tenderness were concerned. (This last comparison by a well-meaning seeker after truth who knew nothing about Woman.) Moreover, he'd been "in" five times for small jobs, and had thoroughly fleshed his teeth in the more pedestrian paths of his profession.

It is curious to note that although Jumbo was hopelessly drunk when he effected this introduction in such happy prose-poetry, he spoke little more than the truth. Can you wonder, then, that when a full-blooded girl like Myra, wife of Tom the Tinker, met a boy so alive, so full of these warm virtues, her heart should turn aside from her man, who possessed only the cold, negative virtues, and go out, naked and unashamed, to Ding-Dong?

You can't wonder. That is precisely what Myra did. She loved Ding-Dong. She loved him for his superb animal body, and also for his clear honesty, strength and absurdly beautiful ideas of playing the game. She hoped she had cured him of those ideas on the night upon which she now let her memory stretch itself. On that night Ding-Dong had come to the little lurking cottage near the raucous waterside, and found her alone; and, he being full of beer and the intent glee of the moment, had tried to kiss Myra. She had repulsed him with a push in the mouth that had made him angry, and he returned to the assault. His large, neat hand had caught the collar of her blouse and ripped it fully open. His free arm had slipped her waist and twisted her off her feet. Then he flew at her as a hawk at its prey. A beast leapt within him and devoured all reason. He crushed her against him, and, as their bodies met in contact, she gasped, resisted his embraces with a brief and futile violence, and, the next moment, he found himself holding a limp and surrendered body.

"Let me go, Ding-Dong," she had cried.

"No; I'll be damned if I do!"

"I'd just hate for you to be damned, Ding-Dong," she had said, nestling to him with an expression at once shy and wild. Then wonder awoke within their hearts, wonder of themselves and of one another and of the world, till, very suddenly, the beer went out of him and he flung her aside, and bowed his head, and turned to the door.

"Where are you going, Ding-Dong?"

"'Eh? Oh, home. I'm sorry. I fergot. I was a bit on, I think. I been a beast."

"No, you 'aven't."

"But I should 'ave been, if I 'adn't remembered. P'r'aps you'll fergive me later on. Bye-bye."

"But you ain't really going?"

"Yerss."

"But—here—going?"

"Yerss."

"Well . . ." She looked at him, then lifted a delicate finger and pulled his ear. "Well . . . you damn fool!"

And somehow he felt that he was.

He felt it so keenly that it seemed to be up to him to repudiate the soft impeachment. So, whenever Tom the Tinker was professionally busy, Ding-Dong, blond and beautiful and strong as some jungle animal, would come to the cottage, and many delirious hours would be passed in the company of the lonely, lovable Myra.

He began to be happy. He began to feel that he really was a man. He was asserting himself. He had stolen another man's wife—sure cachet of masculinity. At the same time he had done nothing dirty, since the man in question didn't want her; had, indeed, often said so in casual asides, uttered in the intervals of driving steel drills through the walls of iron safes.

Yes, Ding-Dong had shown that he was a real man all right; one who could throw himself about with the best. Morally, he swaggered. He thought of the maidens he had loved: poor stuff. He thought of his pals who either were married or did not love at all: poor stuff entirely. It was himself and those like him who were the men. Masculinity, virility only arrived with intrigue.

Myra learned to love him furiously, idiotically. She would have died for him. She knew by the very beat of her pulses when he stood a little away from her that this was her man; this and no other. Come what might of dismay and disaster, this was the man ordained for her. And he . . . did he love her? I wonder. In his own naïve, cleanly simple way he centred his existence on her, but it was rather because she was to him Adventure; fire and salt and all swiftly flavoured things.

Tom the Tinker told her none of his secrets or business affairs. He had the cheapest opinion of women, except for hygienic purposes, and did not believe in letting them know anything about business affairs when they stood in the relationship of The Wife. But from Ding-Dong, in whom Tom did confide, Myra learnt all she wanted to know. It was from him that she had learnt of the Bethnal Green jewellery rampage, which was to come off that night; and if, as has been said, Tom had been able to give his mind to more than one thing at a time, he would have noted the evident disturbance which now held her, and have speculated upon its cause. Its cause happened to be an inspiration which had come to her the moment Ding-Dong, resting in her plaintive arms under the cool order of her autumn-tinted hair, had let drop the plans for that night.

Since the appearance of Ding-Dong in her musty life she had come to hate Tom. She hated him because he had drawn her into the bonds of matrimony, and then had shown her that he regarded her as only a physical necessity. She hated him for his mistrust of her, for his reticence and for the sorry figure he cut against the vibrant Ding-Dong. She was ripe to do him an injury, but, by his silence about his affairs, he gave her no chance. And now Ding-Dong had, all innocently, placed in her hands the weapon by which she could strike him and force him to suffer something of what she had suffered as a matrimonial prisoner. He should have a taste of the same stuff. She knew that once he was nabbed a good stretch was awaiting him—five years at least—since he had long been wanted by the local police. She might, of course, have surrendered him at any time, but that would have meant an appearance in the witness box, and she did not wish to play the rôle of the treacherous wife; much better to let the blow descend from out of the void.

Half-past twelve was the time fixed for the meeting between Ding-Dong and Tom, and it was now ten o'clock. Tom still sprawled by the fire, staring cataleptically at the carpet, and presently Myra languidly stretched herself and got up.

"Got no beer in the house," she said, addressing the kitchen at large. "I'll just pop round to Lizzie's and borrow a couple of bottles."

She swung out of the kitchen, sped swiftly upstairs, found a hat and cloak, and slipped from the house. But she did not go towards Lizzie's. She went into East India Dock Road and across to a narrow courtyard. Leaning against a post at its entrance was a youth of about eighteen, a frayed Woodbine drooping from his lips.

"That you, Monico?" she asked, peering through the gloom.

"You've clicked."

"D'you know where Wiggy is? Go'n find 'im for me."

The youth departed, and presently a greasy figure shuffled out of the courtyard; a figure known and hated and feared in that district; Wiggy, the copper's nark. He looked up at the woman, who had drawn a purple veil across her face. "Wodyeh want?"

She told him. For three minutes she held him in talk. Then she disappeared as swiftly as she had come, disappeared in the direction of Pennyfields. At the corner of Pennyfields is a fried-fish bar. She entered.

"D'you know a boy called Ding-Dong—comes in here every night? Big, fair-haired."

"Yerss, I know 'im."

"Has he been in yet?"

"'Nit. I'm expectin' 'im, though. 'As supper 'ere every night 'bout this time."

"That's right. Well, when he comes, will you tell him—and say it's most particular—that they've changed the time. It was to be half-past twelve, but they've changed it to one o'clock. Just tell 'im that, will you? He'll understand. One o'clock 'stead of half-past twelve. See?"

"Right-o. I'll see 'e gets it."

"Thanks." And homeward she went, calling on the way for the two bottles of beer which had been the ostensible purpose of her errand.

Tom still sat where she had left him, and refused any supper. He was going out, he said, and would have supper with some friends. She needn't sit up for him. So she took the two bottles up to her bedroom and sat in a hammock chair, drinking stout, which she found very comforting, and waiting anxiously for the hour when Tom would depart.

At five minutes to twelve she heard the door slam, and she knew that revenge was very near. Punishment would now swiftly fall upon the hated Tom the Tinker, and freedom would be hers and the joy of Ding-Dong's continual presence. She opened the second bottle and drank to her new life. Oh, she was a smart girl, she knew; she was the wily one; she had 'em all beaten. Life was just beginning for her, and, under the influence of the stout, she dreamed a hazy dream of rejuvenation; how she would blossom into new strength and beauty under the admiring eyes and the careful ministrations of her Ding-Dong. Farewell the dingy little back kitchen. Fare-well the life of slavery and contempt. Farewell the wretched folk among whom she had been forced to live while Tom pursued his dirty work. Hail to the new world and the new life!

Her head nodded, and for a few minutes she dozed. She was awakened by the sound of a creaking window. Then footsteps—stealthy, stuttering steps. They came up the stairway.

Ding-Dong! She knew his step. Her plan had come off. Tom had been nabbed by the cops; Ding-Dong had arrived half-an-hour after the appointed time; had waited for Tom; found that he had not arrived, and so had come to his place to make inquiries. Oh, joy! Now that Tom was taken, nothing that anyone could do could save him; so that it would be left to them only to enjoy the blessed gift that the gods had given to them; and by the time Tom came out again she would have won Ding-Dong entirely for herself, and he would have taken her to Australia or America.

The step stopped at her door, the handle was turned and in walked the intruder. She stared at him for a moment, then a low, nondescript cry burst from her throat: the cry of a cornered animal.

Tom the Tinker came into her bedroom. He was more agitated than she had ever known him to be. He showed no surprise at finding her out of bed. On his shirt, just where his tie failed to cover it, were spots of blood. He sank into a chair.

"Myra, old woman, I'm done. There's been some rough stuff. I 'ad a job on, at Bethnal Green. With Ding-Dong. On'y 'e was late. 'Alf-an-hour late. If 'e'd bin on time we could 'a' done it and fixed our getaway. But 'e was late. And the cops must have 'ad the office. I didn't wait. I went in alone, and when I 'eard the jerry I up and off over the wall at the back, where it was clear. But just as I up and off, old Ding-Dong, 'earing the schlemozzle, come running up, and they copped 'im fair. I slipped round to see, and he lashed out and sent a cop down with a jemmy. Then they drew their whackers and smashed him on the 'ead. He fell kinder sideways, and come with 'is 'ead crack on the kerb. 'E's dead now. Dead. I 'eard it from Paris Pete, who followed 'em up to the station. Dead, 'e is. 'E was a blasted good feller. . . . Well, I levanted, but I reckon they got me taped somehow. I 'it one of the cops—'it 'im 'ard. And now I got to lie under a bit, till it's blown over. I'm all right, I think; they don't know me. I bin too careful alwis. They don't know I b'long 'ere. So I'm all right, if you'll stand in, old woman. You won't let on, will yeh? Nobody knows about it but you and Ding-Dong. And 'e's dead. They'll never git me unless you go back on me. You'll 'ave to play up a bit, cos I sha'n't be able to git about at all for a bit. You'll 'elp us out, old woman, won't yeh? I bin a good 'usban' to yeh, ain't I? I ain't never let yeh want for nothing, 'ave I?" She seemed to catch a sob in his throat. "Ol' Ding-Dong . . ." he stammered. "Blasted good feller. . . . Dead, 'e is. Yeh won't go back on me, will yeh?"

She flung herself back in the hammock and laughed, a high, hollow, staccato laugh, in which was weariness and bitterness.

"Oh . . . that's all right, Tom. Yerss . . . I'll . . . I'll stand in. Oh, but it's damn funny . . ." And she went off into peals of muffled laughter.

OLD JOE

MR. PETER PUNDITT nipped out of his little newsagent's and tobacconist's shop in West India Dock Road, carrying in his hand a large, damp sheet, smelling strongly of the press. This he carefully pasted over a demurely complacent contents bill of *The Telegraph*, and then stepped back to look at it in the grey incertitude of the Limehouse twilight. It read:

PUNDITT'S ONE-HORSE SNIP
One Penny Daily
Is Away from Everything
Who Gave
PAINTED LADY
GOLD CUP?

It was to be noted that Mr. Punditt, from motives of modesty or wariness, refrained from throwing any light on his part in this dubious transaction.

With cocked head and silently whistling lips he contemplated his work, recognising, with some satisfaction, how much more arresting was his bill than that of *Gale's Monday Night Special*, by whose side it stood. He was just about to nip in again, when he heard a weak, erratic step behind him, and, turning, beheld a youth of about twenty, with sallow, pimply face, slack-mouthed and furtive. An unlit Woodbine dropped from his lips.

Little Peter Punditt, the smartest bookie in Limehouse, Poplar and Blackwall, turned swiftly about. "Well?"

"Er—look 'ere, Punditt, o' man, I'm—I'm 'fraid I sha'n't be able to manage anything. Y'see——"

"Oh!" Punditt regarded the weed in front of him with an airy tolerance. "Oh! Yeh can't manage anything, can't yeh? Yer *afraid*, are yeh? . . . Look 'ere, that kind 'o talk is twos into one wiv me. See?"

"Two's into——"

"Yerss. It won't go. It's Punditt what's talking to yeh. Yeh know Punditt's way wiv bilkers, doncher? Before I've finished wiv a bilker he's wishing he'd collected stamps instead."

"Yes, but . . . I mean . . . I . . . It was your tips what I followed. You let me down every time. Every time. You said this last was a cert, and I put me shirt on it, and——"

119

"An' if I did? Who th'ell arst yeh to back 'orses at all? Eh? Did I arst yeh to buy Punditt's One-Horse Snip? Eh? YeH lose yer money, then yeh come whinin' rahnd 'ere wiv a face abaht as cheerful as cold boiled potatoes on a foggy night. Did I arst ye to put yer money on—eh?" His tone changed. "Look 'ere—don't get gay wiv me, me boy. Cos gettin' gay wiv me's about as 'ealthy as monkeying wiv a buzz-saw. See? You just got to settle up. I gave y'an extra fortnight, and it's up today. Lessee . . . Monday, ain't it? Tell yeh what I'll do—an' I don't go as far wiv most people—I'll give yeh two days more. If yeh don't brass up by Wednesday night—then I'll see that yeh get it where the bottle got the cork. That plain enough for yeh?"

He wagged a minatory finger wearing a thick band of mourning in the nail. "Y'know what I can do to you, doncher, sonny? A dozen words out of my mouth, and . . . Wow-wow. You be good, and don't make me do it."

The boy spluttered, with vociferant hands. "No, but, Punditt, o' man, how can I? How can I get it? There ain't no way. I mean——"

"Don't matter a shake of a nannygoat's tail to me where yeh git it or 'ow yeh get it. Yeh got to get it by Wednesday—that's all. Else . . ." He threw his arms to the street, lifted both hands, thumbs protruding upwards. With dramatic pantomime he reversed his hands, thumbs pointing fatefully downwards. "Fumbs up, Punditt. Fumbs down, Perce Sleep. Three quid by Wednesday, mind. Get a sudden rush of brains to the 'ead and perduce it; otherwise . . ." he lingered on the word—"otherwise—I shall behave in a very varicose vein, I can tell yeh."

"No, but, Punditt, I——"

"Suffish. Make a noise like a hoop and roll away!"

From his pallid face the boy expressed the bitter essence of contempt which the weak have for all that is pitiless and strong. His mouth made rude noises. His fingers interpreted them. He went away grieved, for he had no possessions. He slouched away, his feet seeming not in complete accord with his knees. A lurid sunset turned a last sickly smile upon him before it died.

It was Peter Punditt who had spoken, and he knew it was the last word. He knew what Peter could do for him. He knew what Peter knew about a certain affair in Amoy Place.

His floury face, flecked with pimples, slacked some degrees further, and he went miserably down the road. He hated the look of it. He had quarrels with God and man and all creeping things, and his legs loathed the pavement. He was smitten and afflicted. He thought he would like to creep away and die. He thought comfortably upon death, and was rather sorry he had not told Peter that he would throw himself in the river that night. Yes; he could die and leave a note that would put the fair khybosh on old Peter Punditt. Mentally, he wrote the note, showing up old Punditt.

But three quid. . . . Was there as much money anywhere in the world? If only he'd been in regular work now—when he kept the petty cash at the warehouse. . . .

Oh, blast it. It didn't bear thinking about. Blast everybody. He hated the world. He hated the sky. He hated his home and all that was in it. No good going home. No good mooning about the streets. No good in anything, so far as one could see. He stopped near the bridge of the Isle of Dogs and glowered upon the river and upon smoke-stack, rigging and sail.

The evening was at once heartsome and subdued. On the deck of a Nippon the dear, drunken devils of yellow seamen were making soft music on Chinese guitars. A steady frost had settled and, with complete darkness, the usually lowering streets of the Asiatic quarter seemed strangely wide and frank. A fat-faced moon was slowly rising. The waters were swift and limpid, sprinkled with timid stars, and seemed to promise a very blessed time to the weary. On the corner by the dock gates the Blue Lantern shone sharp, like a cut gem. He lounged over the side of the bridge, and, so still was the night, he could almost hear a goods train shunt. It was still enough to bring from a narrow street, flanked by two tremendous walls, a curious sound of *sup-sup, sup-sup*.

Perce Sleep heard it. "Bloody Chinks!" he growled. The next moment the *sup-sup* came from behind him, and a hand fell on his shoulder. A yellow face peered at him. It was old, flabby, steamy.

"'Ullo, li'l Perce!" The words came so musically that one would have said they were sung.

"'Ullo, Chopstick. Gointer buy us a beer?"

"Les. Co'long Shaik Yip. Have plety beer."

"Aw right. Look 'ere, Chinky, I'm in a mess. You're all right for the ready, everyone says. Got a pot o' the dibs, I reckon. Now look 'ere . . . would you . . . I mean . . . will yeh be a sport, and——"

"Ao." Shaik Yip smiled a meaningless Oriental smile. "Perce want money. Ao. Peree and Shaik Yip talk business. Co'long. Co'long."

And they entered the Blue Lantern and ordered two Gypsy's Warnings and some of the Nearer-my-God-to-Thee sandwiches.

*　　*　　*

The Sleep *ménage* was not such as one would turn to happily, when weary, for repose. Perce lived with his stepfather, a paralytic, and the old man's daughter, a "softie." The old man, a mass of helpless flesh, lived in a chair by the fireside. He had been a stevedore in his time, and his great shaggy head, his rolling shoulders, and the long, thick arms, all now as white and motionless as death, told a tale of superb strength in youth. There he sat now, and there he was fed and tended and washed. The only life that had been left him was his voice, and of this there only remained a thin piping, so that he was known locally as Old Joe, after that Fleet Street notability who, every morning at ten-thirty in the Fourth Edition, gives the world his famous treble.

His daughter, a slip of a girl, was the mother of the house. Her face had that arresting beauty sometimes seen in the faces of the vacant-minded. There was nothing of the idiot about her, save in her talk and her simple character. She managed the house, and she managed Old Joe, and she strove hard to manage the waster, Perce.

"Wis'ful," someone had said. "Wis'ful—that's 'ow she looks. Like as if she was wanting to catch 'old of something that ain't there."

As for Perce, he only ate and drank and slept at the house, and had little to do with Fanny, save to borrow coppers from her.

"A wicked boy," piped Old Joe. "That's what 'e is. Never tries to get work. Got one job, and got sacked from that, and ain't done a stroke since. 'Anging about pubs and mixin' wiv wasters. Grr! 'E'll end in gaol, mark what I say. Blast 'im. Arr. . . . Fanny's the good girl. Where'd we all be if it wasn't for Fanny? Looks after us and keeps us all going. Does anything to keep the 'ome together, doncher, me gel? Goes out charing, or does needle-work. Clever wiv 'er needle, she is. But that blasted Perce. Grr! I'd spit on 'im. I'd turn 'im out the 'ouse if I could. But 'e won't go. Cos 'e knows I'm 'elpless and can't do nothing. Not if 'e struck me I couldn't do nothink. An' 'e's nearly done it, oncer twice. The blasted drunken little waster. Gawd—if I'd a-got my strength back—I'd learn 'im. You dunno—nobody dunno—what I've 'ad to put up wiv from 'im—all cos I can't move—an' 'e knows it. Things 'e's said to me. Things 'e's done. Gawd. Dunno what I've a-done that I should 'ave to put up . . ."

Whereupon he would collapse and weep cold tears down his huge white face, and Fanny would run in from her daily work, or drop her sewing, and paw him and talk baby-talk to him.

He was right about Perce, though. Perce was the boy for fancy waist-coats and the private bar. Perce was the boy for the athletic saloon—as an onlooker. Perce was the boy for hanging on the fringe of those who lead the impetuous life. But Perce was never the boy for a fight or an adventure or a woman, or for any indulgence that called for quality. Perce was the complete rotter.

Perce was the boy to glower upon the helpless giant and tell him off. "Oh, shut up," he'd snarl. "You ought to be in a work'ouse, you did. Or else in a play. Cut yer blasted yap, cancher, yer rotten old nuisance!"

And the old man would return, shrilly and tearfully: "I'm sorry, Perce, me boy. But I'm an old man, y'know, and queer. And I sits 'ere all day and all night, and I can't 'elp *feeling* things. I know yer a good boy, really, though yeh do speak sharp sometimes. . . . Arr . . . if only Gawd'd give me back my strength, I could work for all of us. Me, strongest man in London Docks, and now a-sitting 'ere day and night, day and night, day and night."

On the Monday night he did not come home, and Old Joe was wondering where he might be, and hoping to Christ he'd tumbled in the river; and Fanny, too, on Tuesday night, was wondering and laying the supper, and hoping nothing had happened, and assuring Old Joe that Perce was a nice, good boy.

At eight o'clock a step sounded in the cadaverous darkness of Bluegate Lane, and Perce came in. His key rattled in the door, and words passed between him and another. He was heard to wipe his boots—a thing he had never been known to do. He seemed to be walking uncertainly, with many feet.

Then the kitchen door was snatched open by Fanny, the soft, and Perce was heard by her and Old Joe to murmur: "Tha'll be all right."

But only Perce entered the kitchen.

He sank at once into a chair, as though wearied almost to exhaustion. He stretched his legs so that fatigue might express itself in every line of his figure. He lit a Woodbine. Supper was on the table—some bread and pickles and cheese, knives, and a jug of beer. He grabbed the jug to his mouth and drank noisily from it, and angrily, as though he were at last getting his rights from the world.

"Well, old 'un," he tossed at the old man, perfunctorily, by way of salutation. He strove to put warmth and jocularity in the tone, but his face and lips remained stiff and cold. He smacked his hands together. "Ah, well," he observed to the room generally. He looked critically at his hands. "Fingernails want cutting," he remarked inconsequently. Old Joe took no notice of his greeting; did not look at him; seemed to be intent on something known only to himself.

"'Ere, Fanny-baby," called Perce, "want you a minute."

"What you want Fanny for, Percy-boy?"

"Go up t'your bedroom, will yeh, and get those scissors."

"Here's pair scissors here."

"Yes, but . . . I want th'other pair. The small ones in your room."

"'Oo's that in th'ouse?" snapped Old Joe, with pistol-shot explosion. "Someone's in th'ouse. I can feel it!"

"Can't Percy-boy go'mself?" prattled Fanny.

"No—too tired. You go—there's a goo' girl. Then I'll buy you some chocolate biscuits." He looked covertly to right and left.

"Awright. Fanny go. Cho-co-late biscuits!" she sang, to no tune.

"Fanny!" Old Joe bit off the words. "You stop 'ere!"

Perce slewed round. "Whaffor, old 'un? Why can't she go?"

"'Cos I don't want 'er to. Fanny—stop. Stop 'ere!"

"Whaffor, daddie dear? Why daddie not want Fanny to go?"

"Cos I . . . I . . . want yeh. There's something . . . something going on. I . . . don't understand. I can feel it. All round, like. Perce, me boy, what you looking like that for? Eh? Whassup? You got some game on, Perce. Oo's that in th'ouse?"

Perce affected not to hear. "Go on, Fan, there's goo' girl. Up yeh go. Old man's got the fair fantods tonight."

"Fanny!" It was a shrill scream, strained with effort. "Don't you go. It's yer old dad tells yeh. For the love of God Almighty, don't go. There's something . . . I know. I can feel it. I can tell it by that beast's face. What's 'e want cutting 'is nails this time o' night?"

Fanny ran to him, crooning. "Daddie musn't call Percy a beast. Percy good brother to Fanny. Going to buy Fanny chocolate biscuits."

"Yerss," said Perce, "don't call me names like that else I'll make a rough 'ouse, I tell yeh. If yeh wasn't a blasted cripple I'd clump yeh one fer that. See?"

The great Windsor chair in which the old man was imprisoned shook with his efforts to raise his piping treble. "Fanny—Fanny—stop! I tell yeh, stop! For the love of the Lord Jesus Christ, stay 'ere."

"No. Fanny go get scissors. You not good, daddie. You call brother beast," And, with a beautiful smile through which nothing could be even divined of the empty mind it clothed, she slipped through the door and disappeared up the stairs, laughing and singing, "Cho-co-late biscuits!"

The old man moaned. His head dropped and wagged. His mouth spat toads in the shape of curses at Perce. Perce moved away. His face was slate-grey. He was limp, and looked as self-controlled as a rabbit about to be slaughtered. He peered into the passage, then passed out, and the old man heard his step ascending the stair. He caught the lazy hum of voices busy in talk. He heard two words, in syrupy accents, which he understood: *Pao-pei!* He heard Fanny's baby accents. "Can't find scissors! Someone's taken scissors. Can't find candle, neether. Someone's taken matches, too."

He heard Perce's voice. "Wait half-a-jiff, Fan. Can't yeh find the matches? 'Ere . . . Fan . . . 'ere. Listen. Something nice for yeh, if yeh'll be a good girl. 'Ere . . . lots of choc'late biscuits. Look . . . no; can't 'ave them yet. In a minute or two. 'Ere, don't be silly. . . . No . . . Just . . . Go on. . . . No, it isn't. . . ."

A door clicked, and swiftly Perce descended the stairs, and entered the kitchen. He was breathing rapidly.

"What you go up for?" whined Old Joe. "Eh? Oh, I know there's something . . . something going to 'appen. I can feel it."

Perce swaggered. "You blasted invalids are alwis feeling and seeing things that ain't there. You'll see blue monkeys next."

Old Joe rocked himself. From above there came a second click; moving feet. There was a moment's silence, then, shattering it, a soft cry, a long-drawn whoosh and a muffled scream. The scream was but a single note, and thereafter came only nondescript low noises.

The old man mouthed and gibbered. He heaved himself idiotically in his chair. "Oh, my Gawd. If I'd a-got my strength. Owh. What are they doing to 'er? What you up to, yeh bleeding swine! Owh. If Gawd don't strike you dead for this. Owh . . . hark at 'er . . . my lamb . . . my . . . O Lord Jesus Christ, save 'er!

"Oh, Perce, dear . . . go up and stop 'em. Stop their devils' work. Fanny! Fanny! What they doing to yeh?" The great white cheeks sagged in many creases as he fought for movement. The heavy arms on each side of the chair dangled like puppets. "Oh, Gawd, if I could find out what they was doing. Oh, if I'd a-got my strength!"

"Oh, shut yeh blasted mag, for Christ's sake!" Perce dropped into a chair and sat scared and pensive. Three long gasps came down the stairway—rhythmic, regular, punctuated by a dull noise.

"Perce! Oh, if I'd a-got my strength . . . oh, I'd squeeze yer throat. Owh. I could a-killed you wiv one 'and. Kill 'im, Gawd! Kill 'im! Strike the bleeder dead! Or give me back me arms. O-o-wh!"

And now he blubbered and whined and entreated. Big tears ran down the doughy face. He writhed. "Oh, Perce—be a good boy and stop 'em before it's too late. I can't bear it. It'll drive me mad. I can't listen to it. . . .

Oh, stop yer devils' work and bring 'er down. My bonny li'l gel. . . . Owh.
I'd learn 'em to put their slimy 'ands on 'er . . . If I'd a-got my strength,
I'd—"

"Well, you 'aven't. So shut yeh silly face." Perce got up and lit another
Woodbine. He looked down uneasily at Old Joe, yet confident of security
in the utter helplessness of the living corpse. "Yeh wasting yeh breath, that's
what yeh doing. There's nothing to make a fuss about. Nothing. She ain't
being murdered. And they ain't doing the other thing, what you think. It's
on'y a bit o' fun. Yeh needn't worry. I take me oath she ain't being . . . you
know, or anything. She'll 'ave forgotten all about it five minutes after. On'y
a bit o' sport, that's all. I got *some* principles, though you think I ain't, y'old
perisher. All yer swearing don't do no good, and yer fists can't. And yer
making a blasted fuss about nothing at all. Nothing at all. So—"

He broke off. For a moment he wondered why. He had stopped
instinctively because something else had stopped: the little cries and gasps.

A door clicked. A step sounded. Someone came downstairs. The old
man rolled from side to side, slobbering and dribbling. He had the appearance of one very drunk. Round the half-shut door slid a large, stooping
Chinky, flashily dressed in East End ready-mades. Under the yellow skin
was a slow flush. His eyes sparkled. His thin, black hair was disordered.

He moved towards Perce. Three coins jingled from his hand to the
stretched hand of Perce. Old Joe wobbled. He saw them; they were gold. He
jerked his head forward and let out—so suddenly that both men jumped—a
high-pitched shout, louder and stronger than any he had before been able
to produce.

"Yeh damn devils! Wotter yeh done to 'er? Oh, Gawd, if I'd a-got—"

The Chink turned about and shuffled amiably to the door. Over his
shoulder he looked at Perce and made a leering remark, accompanied by a
licking of the lips. They nodded heads together.

Curious noises came from the chair at the fire; noises like the low
sucking of a wolf. The old man's jaw had fallen fully open and disclosed
yellow teeth. His head rolled no longer; it moved in jerks, which grew
shorter and shorter.

"My—little—gel . . ." snarled the lips. "O Lord Jesus Christ, 'elp a
man!"

"Blasted o' fool," said Perce explanatorily. "Alwis 'aving chats wiv
Gawd about something." He took another Woodbine, lit it, and strove to
appear casual. His lips were white and his grubby hand shook.

A violent tremor spread along the flabby body of Old Joe. His head was motionless and was turned towards the table. Something seemed to be calling him in that direction; and, as they nodded and whispered, suddenly the Chink, looking across Perce's shoulder, gave a sharp cry and his immobile face was lit with horror.

"Dekko!"

Perce obeyed sharply. And he saw the giant corpse standing on its feet, towering above him, one huge arm stretched to his own white gills, the other, in the joy of returned strength, clutching the long, lean knife from the supper-table.

THE END

Printed in the United States
44929LVS00004B/177